SYSTEMA PARADOXA

ACCOUNTS OF CRYPTOZOOLOGICAL IMPORT

VOLUME 19
ICE MUSIC
A TALE OF QALUPALIK

AS ACCOUNTED BY ROBERT E. WATERS

NEOPARADOXA
Pennsville, NJ
2024

PUBLISHED BY
NeoParadoxa
A division of eSpec Books
PO Box 242
Pennsville, NJ 08070
www.especbooks.com

ISBN: 978-1-956463-51-4
ISBN (ebook): 978-1-956463-50-7

Interior Design: Danielle McPhail
www.sidhenadaire.com

Cover Art: Jason Whitley
Cover Design: Mike and Danielle McPhail, McP Digital Graphics
Interior Illustration: Jason Whitley

Copyediting: Greg Schauer and John L. French

DEDICATION

FOR ERIC FLINT
(1947-2022)

PROLOGUE

Elisapie heard music, and she smiled.

It wasn't the Inuit throat music she had heard at her father's town hall in Anchorage a few months ago. Truth be told, she didn't really like, or even understand, throat music. It had a kind of breathy sound to it, like someone gasping hard, then singing, and then gasping hard again. The voice Elisapie heard now had a strong, high harmony. The notes winding their way through her frost-covered windows rose high and then dropped, then high again, then another drop, all in perfect rhythm. It was as if the person singing called to her, inviting her to come. Come where? She did not know. Outside? Yes, maybe.

Could she go outside? She wasn't supposed to; wasn't allowed. Her father and brother had already left for the morning. Out ice fishing on Kenai Lake, like they had done for many years now, when Father felt it was necessary to be "a faithful Alaskan," as he called it. Father was a very important man. A "senator" for the United States of America. The first Inuit to serve in that "great deliberative body." Elisapie didn't really know what a senator was, nor did she care at the moment. All that mattered now was the voice and its beautiful notes.

She pushed her covers away and climbed out of the bottom bunk. Her brother Hanta had insisted that he be in the top bunk, as he always did. He wasn't there right now, and Elisapie paused a moment to consider climbing the small wooden ladder at the foot of the bed and bouncing on Hanta's mattress just for fun. Finally, to be on top for once! But no. Not now. Maybe later, before he got back from his "big boy" fishing trip.

Elisapie pushed her feet into her slippers and grabbed her coat and hat from the coat rack in the corner. She did not bother changing into regular clothes or pulling on her boots. The music, the voice, told her that what she was already wearing was fine. *Just come… come to me…*

But could she? Some of Daddy's bodyguards had gone with him and Hanta to provide protection. They were out there now on Kenia Lake, many miles downstream, sitting around a hole that they had cut into the ice, waiting for a bite. But there were still a couple of guards in the kitchen. Elisapie could see the kitchen light through the crack in her door. She could hear the muffled voices of the guards sitting there at the kitchen table, sipping coffee, laughing at their own jokes. Quietly, of course, for Mother was still asleep down the hall. Would they see Elisapie if she casually, without noise, slipped out of her room and walked to the front door of the cabin? She wasn't sure, but the beautiful voice ringing in her ears, through her mind, encouraged her to try.

She opened the door quickly and stepped out into the hallway. She waited. The guards saw and heard nothing. She took another step, and then another, and another, until she passed the kitchen and scampered to the door. Elisapie smiled. *Easy-peasy,* she thought, an expression she had learned from the kids at the private school that she and Hanta attended. Easier than she thought it would be. But the voice, now sounding so confident and angelic, never had a worry. *I knew you could do it,* it said, moving up and down the scale of notes effortlessly. Elisapie couldn't help but marvel at its tone. *Beautiful… just beautiful.*

As are you, Elisapie.

She smiled again and reached the door. The doorknob was cold, and Elisapie realized that she had forgotten to put on her gloves. She thought about going back to her room, but that might alert the guards. The beckoning voice grew stronger in her mind. She ignored the cold, turned the doorknob slowly, heard the faint click of the lock, and opened the door.

It was bitter outside. An overnight snow had blown through. It was gone now, but the wind remained strong. She heard the voice even better now that the door was open. She paused a moment to listen but realized that she couldn't stand there in the gap for long. The guards would feel the cold air and wonder why.

She looked over her shoulder to see if the guards or her mother stirred. Nothing. *Good.* She opened the door a few cracks more and stepped outside.

The cold wasn't so bad now that she was out of the cabin. The wind wasn't so strong and not so bitter. Odd, but she felt a warm tingle in her hands and arms, her face, her neck, and shoulders. The cascade of warmth matched the tempo and grace of the voice, and it made her feel good, happy, wanted.

Come now, Elisapie. Come to me…

To me was across the lightly-snow-dusted driveway and down to the river. Elisapie looked back at the cabin door, saw no one, then stepped down the few steps of the cabin and into the driveway. Only a guard vehicle remained in the driveway; the other guard car and their family SUV were gone, off before daylight on that fishing trip. She could still see the tracks where the cars had been parked. She stepped over them quickly, unconcerned about slipping and falling on her face. That would not happen. The voice would not allow it.

How could she describe the voice? It had changed now that she stood outside. A slightly muffled tone, as if the person singing was behind something, a door or a window. But the notes were perfect, "synchronous" as Mother might say. A perfect tone, moving from head voice to chest voice so effortlessly that it was difficult to know when the transition occurred. It had a different *feel* to it now, more stressful, more insistent, more dire, as if it were calling for help, for rescue.

Elisapie moved quickly, scampering across the driveway and down the small embankment toward the river. Kenai Lake was long, and it stretched out from Riverside Lodge eastward until it became a big body of water. Her father and brother had always done their ice fishing closer to where Kenai became a real lake. They were miles away right now. In her heart, Elisapie wished they were closer. She had been forbidden to go to the riverside alone for fear of her falling through the ice. *Should I go there?* she wondered, but the voice gave her no choice.

She walked down the wooded incline to the bank of the Kenai. The ground at the water's edge was wet, muddy, a little crackly from overnight frost. Hers and Hanta's boot prints were still in the mud from yesterday's walk. She could go to the lake with her brother, but not alone. They had tramped in the mud and had skipped rocks. Hanta had fallen once, and Elisapie had laughed. Hanta had pushed her away, and she had fallen in the mud too. In the end, they both laughed. It was a good time.

Now here she was, on the bank, the water of the Kenai rippling below the thin ice on the surface, and the voice called to her again.

Come to me… save me.

Elisapie took a step onto the ice. She paused, picked up a rock instead, and tossed it as far as she could across the smooth, clear surface. The rock bounced and popped and slid across the ice, making a rumbling sound that seemed to almost match the colorful voice that sang to her. It was clear now where the voice came from: just a few feet out from where she stood.

The rock slid to a stop. There was a pause in the singing. The wind blew across Elisapie's face as light snow began to fall again.

The rock suddenly skipped, seemingly on its own, bouncing and sliding once more across the ice. A knocking sound replaced the music, and Elisapie could see the rock bounce again, again, and again, as a hard, insistent knocking came from below, as if someone were rapping on a door. Elisapie's heart leapt and she dared take a step back.

Come to me, the voice said again, its tone commanding, like her mother's. *Save me.*

Elisapie stepped onto the ice. She was small and thin, so the ice held her firmly. She looked again toward the cabin. She saw no one, so she kept walking carefully, slowly, across the thin ice toward the rock and the incessant tapping beneath the surface.

She kind of liked it, moving on the ice. Slippery, but fun. Why Father and Mother were so afraid of her going out here, she did not know. She was fine. She took another step and another, and finally, she reached the rock.

Come closer…

Elisapie knelt on the slick surface, the frozen water cold against her knees. She looked down at the ice and saw her reflection; there was enough sunlight now that she could see herself clearly. Her dark hair long and wavy, her face smooth and shiny. She smiled.

A greyish-green face rose up from the depth of the lake, pressed against the ice, and smiled back. A sallow face, faded and wrinkled, like the face of Elisapie's grandmother when she had passed away, though hers hadn't been green or grey. The eyes were hollow, like two tiny, twinkling diamonds in the dark. A tiny nose. A soulful expression, withered, but still alive.

The grey-green woman widened her mouth, revealing a line of sharp, jagged yellow teeth.

Save me, Elisapie. Save me.

"Save you?"

Yes.

"From what?"

From dying.

"How… how do I do that?"

The face butted against the underside of the ice. *Come on an adventure with me.*

There was no chance for Elisapie to answer, even if she could. The ice cracked, then shattered. Before she could move out of the way, the green woman burst through, first her face, followed by her arms, long and thin, but powerful. Her bony fingers, tipped with sharp black nails, reached out to Elisapie and grabbed her.

She screamed and struggled against the green woman's grasp. She punched and clawed at the arms. The beautiful voice that had called her to the riverbank was gone. In its place, the harsh, angry growl of a beast.

As the ice broke beneath her, Elisapie reached out toward the bank, toward the cabin, her mother. The woman's black nails tore through her pajama top and ripped a piece away. Elisapie cried out for her brother, her father, but the only one to answer was one of the guards standing on the embankment, yelling her name.

The guard raised his pistol and pointed it toward her. The pistol sounded, and the woman's ashen arms wrapped around Elisapie tighter, vise-like.

Elisapie yelped and heard another pistol shot as she disappeared beneath the ice.

Chapter One

Sitting at her lunch table, Chimalis Burton looked at her watch for the fifth time and rolled her eyes. Her partner, Luiz Vasquez, was late — as usual. But, perhaps this time, she would be more forgiving. Luiz was conducting preliminary research on the infamous Pope Lick Creek Monster from Kentucky, a part-man, part-goat, part-sheep creature who had apparently caused some hideous deaths recently at a railroad bridge spanning said creek. Chimalis rolled her eyes again. She had no desire to confront *another* goat-like creature so soon after vanquishing *El Cadejo* at a junkyard in Texas. That mission had been both mentally and physically draining. *I should just send Luiz to take care of this one*, she thought as she forked around her salad looking for scrumptious croutons to spear. She chuckled to herself. *Another good reason to have an assistant: delegate, delegate, delegate.*

Luiz entered the cafeteria in a flurry of self-deprecating waves and apologies. "I'm sorry, I'm sorry," he said, grabbing a tray, pouring a glass of iced tea, and taking a pre-made turkey club from the counter. He placed them all on the tray and sat down opposite Chimalis. "Sorry so late, boss. It's such a pain in the *culo* speaking with small-town officials."

"They didn't give you a hard time, did they?"

Luiz huffed. "Once they discovered I was with the FBI-VPA, they clammed up right quick and barely gave me any actionable information."

A lot of the citizenry of the United States didn't understand, or appreciate, the work that the Federal Bureau of Investigations of Violent Paranormal Activity did on a daily basis.

Chimalis took a bite of her salad. She both heard and felt the deeply satisfying crunch of a crouton. "What *did* you learn?"

"Not as much as I had hoped." Luiz took a bite from his club sandwich before continuing. "Contact with this Pope Lick creature can apparently cause mania and fear. They say it draws people to the bridge through hypnosis and forces them to jump to their deaths."

"Oh, God!" Chimalis said, dropping her fork into her salad. "It's *El Cadejo* all over again!"

Luiz nodded. "More or less, though we'll only be dealing with one creature this time. Not two brothers intent on settling personal scores."

If she was going to say something, now was the time. She took another quick bite of her salad, placed her fork gently alongside her bowl, and said, "Luiz… I'd like you to take care of this matter."

Luiz paused mid-chew. He looked a little silly sitting there, staring at her with a wad of turkey in his mouth. He suddenly realized his absurdity, chewed, swallowed, and said, "Really? You want *me* to handle it? All by myself?"

Chimalis shrugged. "Why not? You've been with the Bureau a couple years now, and you've always done well by me. You have a strong understanding of cryptids, and your knowledge and skill base are improving daily. You're ready."

Odd, but she felt a tinge of sorrow as she said those last few words. Of course, Luiz *was* ready. He'd been ready to be assigned his own cases for quite a while. But it felt to Chimalis like she was putting her son on the school bus for the first time or waving goodbye as he drove off to college.

They grow up so fast…

Luiz sat quietly for a minute, blinking furiously, obviously rolling the idea around in his head. Finally, he said, "But, what about Halsey? He asked you specifically to investigate the matter."

Chimalis stabbed another crouton, shrugged. "No, he asked us *both* to investigate it. But I'm the chief investigator of the matter, so I can assign anyone I want."

She was about to continue when Halsey walked in. "And speak of the devil," she said, looking past Luiz at her boss, James Halsey, Special Agent in Charge (SAC) of the Colorado FBI field office. He was, as always, dressed immaculately but his expression was one of concern. He'd forgotten to shave this morning, Chimalis noticed. A rare event indeed.

"Special Agent Halsey," Chimalis said, gesturing to the third chair at their table. "Please, have a seat. Luiz was just about to choke on a wad of turkey."

"Yes," Halsey said, "that's very funny." He thumbed behind him toward the hallway. "Agents Burton, Vasquez... may I see you both for a moment? In my office, please?"

"Yeah, we're almost finished here. Give us a sec, and we'll be right there."

Halsey shook his head, blinked a couple of times. "No, right now."

Chimalis furrowed her brow. "Why the rush?"

Halsey sighed, pinched his eyes together, rubbed his reddening face. "A senator's daughter has gone missing. We need to talk... now."

Chimalis had heard about the case, of course. Since it had happened to an important member of Congress, the event had broadcasted everywhere, on every online, streaming, and regular TV news channel. The girl had fallen through the ice on Kenai Lake in Alaska. Federal and local law enforcement were at the scene searching for her body. The matter was being handled. So, why did Chimalis have to meet with SAC Halsey about it?

He described the situation as she and Luiz took seats in his office. "Elisapie Cooke, age eight, daughter of Senator Philip Cooke from Alaska, apparently wandered out of her family's rented cabin at Riverside Lodge and walked on to thin ice before falling through and drowning. Local law enforcement is searching the lake to retrieve her body."

"Yes, I know all this," Chimalis said, rather annoyed at having to hear the obvious and not finishing her delicious salad. Her stomach growled. "Why are we here, in Denver, talking about it?"

Halsey put up his finger for pause. "That is the official, *public* version of the story. There's more to it."

Halsey opened his laptop, waited a moment while its screen activated, then turned it toward Chimalis and Luiz. The scruffy face of a disheveled man forced a meager smile and a nod on-screen. "Hello."

Chimalis sat up straight in her chair and nodded back. "Senator Cooke... I'm so sorry for your loss, sir." She motioned to Luiz. "This is my assistant, Agent Luiz Vasquez. And I'm—"

"I know who you are," Senator Cooke blurted. Chimalis could hear the anxiety, the desperation in his voice. His throat crackled with exhaustion, dryness. "Everyone knows who you are."

Not an entirely accurate statement, but Chimalis let it go. She waited for the senator to continue. He seemed reluctant to do so. Finally, he sighed and said, "My daughter did not drown, Agent Burton. As Halsey indicated, that's the official, public statement, put out there to keep the matter calm, to keep the media — and more importantly, *social* media — from blowing the matter out of proportion. We must investigate this situation quietly, Agent Burton, to keep it out of the public eye."

Chimalis nodded. "Investigate what exactly, sir?"

Senator Cooke sighed again, dropped his gaze, then looked up. "My daughter Elisapie did not drown, Agent Burton. She was abducted."

Halsey chimed in. "A member of Senator Cooke's private security detail claims to have seen the senator's daughter walk out onto the ice. He tried reaching her, but before he even got to the bank, he claims that some… frail, human-like creature broke through the ice, grabbed the girl, and pulled her under. He fired a couple rounds toward the creature, but—"

"He didn't hit the girl, I hope?" Luiz asked.

Senator Cooke shook his head, cleared his throat. "No, he fired above the creature, to try to scare it. It did not work."

"This is obviously a cryptid matter," Halsey said.

If true, then a United States senator wouldn't dare state something like that in public, lest he be ridiculed or, worse, primaried in an upcoming election.

Senator Cooke coughed, winced.

Poor guy.

"Agent Burton," he said, "it's my understanding that you are an expert on Native American cryptids. That is why I have asked for you specifically. I want you and Agent Vasquez to come and find my daughter. I believe my guard when he says she was abducted. I cannot bear the thought of her drowning. I cannot — my wife cannot — accept that. My daughter's alive, Agent Burton. I want you to find her and kill the vile creature that took her."

The room silenced. Everyone was staring at her, including Senator Cooke. Chimalis glanced up at her boss. He nodded. She knew what that meant. *I've no choice. Even if I tried to refuse, I'd be ordered to do so.*

"Very well," she said, nodding, and standing. She turned toward Luiz. "I guess Kentucky will have to wait."

Luiz shook his head and smiled. "No worries, boss."

She turned back toward Senator Cooke. "Very well, Senator. We'll be there. But I want to warn you, sir: I may be an expert on Native American cryptids, but I don't know anything about Inuit culture or mythology."

Chapter Two

That wasn't entirely true. Chimalis knew some things about the Inuit. She knew that the North Alaskan, Canadian, and Greenlandic indigenous peoples often referred to as "Eskimos" were descendants from the so-called Thule people, who spread eastward from western Alaska across the Arctic, displacing other indigenous cultures along the way. She knew that Inuit spiritualism was based on animist principles: all things had spirits. Many Inuit communities included an *angakkuq*, or shaman, who served as a healer and psychotherapist, tending wounds and offering meaningful advice and guidance to those under great mental stress. She knew about the kinds of clothing that they wore: close-hooded parkas and fur trousers; the kinds of weapons that they used on whale and seal hunts: spears, harpoons, bows. She had even heard (and enjoyed) their throat music. Yes, indeed, Chimalis knew a lot about the Inuit.

But she didn't know a damn thing about their cryptids.

She could conveniently blame that on her parents. The late Mr. and Mrs. Burton had been FBI-VPA agents as well, although her dad had also served as an MI6 agent for the British Secret Intelligence Service. Mom was a Zuni native specializing in cryptids of the American Southwest. They had been all over the Americas searching for and, if lucky, eliminating cryptids that threatened the well-being of "civilized" society. Dad had even spent time in Central America back in the early 1980s searching for *El Cadejo*. They knew their stuff, and the library that Chimalis stood in right now was a monument to that dedicated service.

Except that they had never researched or were assigned any VPA missions above the Canadian border. Nothing, absolutely nothing, in their library gave any mention of Inuit cryptids. Yes, there were basic scholarly books about Inuit culture, and at least one of their sources indicated that the Alaskan Inuit were called Iñupiat. With all this information at hand, Chimalis could, at least, arrive in Anchorage and begin their investigation without seeming clueless. But she needed more information… a lot more.

She pulled her cell phone from her pocket and punched in a number. It rang three times, then, "Yes, may I help you?"

It wasn't the voice she was expecting. "Ah, hello. This is Agent Chimalis Burton, FBI-VPA. May I speak with Father Diego de Seña, please?"

"I'm sorry, Ms. Burton," the woman said, "but Father de Seña is in the hospital with RSV."

"Is he okay?" Chimalis asked, feeling a tightness in her chest.

"Oh, yes, he's fine. He's recovering well, but he's not able to speak right now. If you care to leave a message, I can—"

"Yes, tell him that Bluebird called; he knows who I am. Nothing serious, just to chat. Please let him know I wish him well, and I'll call back once he's out of the hospital."

She hung up and slid the phone across the long table in the center of the library. Not only could she not acquire the needed information from Father de Seña, she now had to worry about his health.

Damn!

If she had time, she'd grab a search warrant and fly down to Corpus Christi to rifle through the priest's library. There, she would most certainly learn what she needed to know about Inuit cryptids; his library was just as valuable, if not more so, than her parents'. But she didn't have that kind of time. Right now, Luiz was booking travel to Anchorage, and she was scheduled to return to Denver for the flight by 8PM. This quick little junket back home to find crucial information had proven useless.

Well, not entirely.

Rising from the table, Chimalis grabbed her phone and left the room, locking the door to the library behind her. She turned and looked up at the mantel above her electric fireplace. There sat her Zuni ritual knife, given to her by her mother, sheathed comfortably in a leather holster. She smiled.

According to Mom, the knife had been forged by the Zuni twin gods of war, Ahayu'da. The gods of war themselves had been created by Awonawilona, the Sun God. Mother had always been a little hazy on exactly when and why Ahayu'da had forged the blade, and for what purpose. In truth, Chimalis had always chalked up the legend to myth and hearsay, handed down generation to generation until the blade finally, for some unknown reason, landed in her family's possession. One thing was true, though: the knife had the power to vanquish cryptid life-forces, and it was a critical part of her ability to serve as a VPA agent.

She eyed the hilt and its emblazoned symbols of defeated cryptids, including the most recent dual symbols of *El Cadejo*. The symbols were not lit with fire as they often were when the blade absorbed another cryptid spirit. They were quiet, cold, non-threatening. Rather lovely in their silent repose, a far cry from the horrifying souls they represented.

She took the knife off the mantel and tucked it into her purse. She always felt more confident, more assured of herself with it on her person. It was like a third arm, a security blanket, and hopefully, it would fulfil its duty as it had done countless times in the past.

"Time to go," she said aloud as she headed to the front door. "Alaska, here I come."

Nipi remembered the warning her *anaana*, her mother, had given her when she was the same age as the girl resting quietly now in the pouch of her *amautik*, her parka. The child was wrapped comfortably in a spell that Nipi had woven around the girl's body to ensure that she did not drown. Drowning would be bad, for if she drowned her essence, her youthful energy, could not be absorbed, consumed. And that would be *really* bad… bad, bad, bad.

The girl was heavy, heavier than Nipi ever remembered a child feeling in her pouch. She knew why: she grew old. One hundred and thirty years now. Was that right? Hard to remember. Maybe much older. The years blurred from one to the next, adrift in this cold soup of water, letting the flow of this river or that lake, that ocean, carry her from place to place, and all the shorelines blending together like the distant memories from when Nipi was real, whole, alive, human. Now all she did was feast on children just to survive.

Do not go to the water alone, Nipi… that was the warning her *anaana* had given her. She had not listened.

Where to take the girl? Nipi knew where. Not the most ideal location under Kenai Lake. It was too close to the place that humans called Drifters Lodge. But she had used the cave before, and she had never had any trouble pulling a young boy or girl down to it, taking them from her *amautik* and tucking them under rocks so that their young bodies would not float to the top. Exposure was the enemy. Discovery would be her death.

But she *was* dying, wasn't she? One hundred and thirty years of feeding along the Alaskan, Canadian, Russian, and Greenland coasts. One child like the girl on her back could last her months. How wonderful! But somehow, Nipi knew that this girl would not be enough.

Nipi dove deeper, feeling the weight of the girl push her down, down until she was afraid that she'd not be able to stop before slamming into the bottom. Before she struck, Nipi reached out with her long, thin arms and pushed herself free from the rocks and slime on the river floor. The cave was near. She could not see its entrance from where she was located, despite rays of sunlight shining through the cold water, leading her forward to security as they often did. She could not see the cave, but she could sense it, like the mouth of a big Arctic char waiting for food. Nipi herself was famished, ravenous. She could not wait any longer.

The mouth of the cave sparkled with faint sunlight. Nipi blew through the entrance, narrower than she remembered it, but not so tight as to threaten to rip her *amautik* off and kill the child. The bitter water rushed across Nipi's sallow green face. She was used to it, but now it felt different somehow, colder, as if her years of swimming through frigid waters were finally catching up to her. She frowned, her thin, bitter lips covering a row of jagged yellow fangs and chipped teeth.

She burst through the cave tunnel and into a small, irregularly shaped room; more like a hole carved out of the lake floor. Big enough, though, for her and her new friend. Nipi always considered her captives her friends. She would share with them the memories of her life, the good times and the bad, and they would pay back her kindness by giving her sustenance, warmth, vibrancy. This girl would do the same, in her own way. Every captive was different, but Nipi had faith in this one. The girl was bright, energetic, inquisitive. All the traits that made the feeding more enjoyable, more fulfilling.

Nipi slowed herself and came to rest on a large stone in the back of the room. She took off her *amautik,* carefully cradling the child so she would not pop out of the pouch and strike the wall or floor of the room and awaken, only to drown. With her remaining strength, Nipi reinforced the spell she had cast on the girl to ensure her safety, and then pulled her free from the parka. She let the girl float in front of her, for just a moment.

She was a beautiful child. Nice, long dark hair, a smooth, clean face, inquisitive eyes, though they were closed now. Gone was the fearful expression the girl had worn as Nipi pulled her under the ice and into her pouch. The spell had closed them and had given the girl—*Elisapie, was that her name?*—a quiet disposition, a soft, pleasing contentment. A hint of smile as if the girl were adrift in a sweet dream. Nipi shuddered. Feeding on this child would be so, so wonderful.

Nipi pulled the girl down until they were face to face. It was like seeing her reflection in a mirror. Her hair had been a little lighter and not so long as this girl's, but her angelic face... yes, her face. So, so similar. Nipi regretted having to feed on her, but only for a moment. The cold, nearly unbearable mucky water around them made her old bones ache. She could not waste any more time on nostalgia.

She put her arm around the girl and pulled her closer until their bodies nearly touched. Nipi then laid her other hand on the girl's face, closed her eyes and reached into the girl, focusing on the heart and the sweet, lovely red blood pumping slowly through Elisapie's clear veins. Wonderful, all so wonderful. Nipi focused on the coursing of the blood.

Yes! Yes! Nipi shivered as the girl's essence, her energy, tingled across her long, dry fingers. A warm glow spread from her hand, up her arm, through her chest, and into her face. It had been years since she had felt such a rush of heat through her body. She wanted to cry. She pressed her hand harder against the girl and felt another burst of energy plump her skin, flatten her wrinkles.

Nipi wallowed in the sensation.

She pulled away quickly. *No!* She could not indulge like this for so long. Doing so would kill the girl right off, and then where would she be? No. That was enough for now.

The girl was still asleep, still floating there before her. Her cheeks were not so smooth now, her hair not so dark and silky. In their place, clear signs of sudden aging: sunken cheeks, dry, cracked hair. Thankfully, her hair had not turned grey. That was good. Nipi had pulled away before she had drunk too much. Good. Very good.

But it was clear now that this girl would not be enough. Nipi had fed for only a few seconds and look what had happened. Two, maybe three, more feedings and the girl would be gone, a dried husk, a piece of driftwood. Nipi grew old; her body needed more energy just to function.

Nipi collected herself. She then grabbed the girl and pulled her to the cave floor. She dug a small space out of the mud so that the girl's sleeping body would rest peacefully under the rocks. She laid the girl down and cuddled her up as nice and neat as if she were sleeping beneath her own blankets. Nipi then pulled rocks over and laid them carefully on the girl until only her face showed.

I must find another, Nipi thought as the energy of the girl still coursed through her veins.

Nipi rubbed the girl's forehead in appreciation before turning and swimming out of the cave.

CHAPTER THREE

"As I'm sure you are aware, Agent Burton," said Agent Wallace, sitting in front of her in the limousine, "our staff here in Anchorage is small. Our VPA branch is even smaller. In fact, I'm really the only agent dedicated to the VPA."

"Yes, I'm aware of that, Agent Wallace. Thank you."

Chimalis crossed her legs for more comfort. She was quite impressed by the mode of transportation in which she and Luiz currently resided. It was rare for agents to be picked up by limo at the airport. In a bullet-proof black sedan? Yes. FBI van? Of course. But a car of this nature was rare. Obviously, Senator Cooke was putting some serious money and effort into finding his daughter. Totally understandable, though placing so much light on the matter by picking up FBI agents in a stretch might draw unwarranted scrutiny by the media, which, she knew, Senator Cooke did not want. What kind of credibility would a United States senator have if word got out that he believed that a lake monster had snatched his daughter?

She'd researched the senator when she was preparing for this case. He was Inuit, at least partially. She did not know his full heritage, but she had uncovered enough of his background to know the kind of man he was. For an Inuit like Senator Cooke to admit that he believed in cryptids would not be so strange or problematic here in Alaska. In Washington, DC? That would be a problem.

As she settled in, Luiz handed her a folder. Elisapie Cooke's file. The first thing Chimalis saw when she flipped it open was an evidence bag holding a torn piece of flannel. It threw her for a moment. The harsh reality of that bit of soiled cloth. She thumbed through the rest of the file, looking at pictures provided by Elisapie's father. Chimalis smiled. She was a beautiful child, ear-to-ear smiles, bright eyes, energetic. In one picture, her dark hair was braided and twisted into a bun on the back of her head. In another, she wore traditional ceremonial clothing designed for Inuit girls. That picture had been taken recently; just two weeks ago. Chimalis smiled again. She ran a tender finger over the girl's image and marveled over the colors and textures of the costume.

Don't worry, honey… we'll find you.

Assuming, of course, that the senator's security man was correct about the abduction. "Fill me in on the investigation," Chimalis said, closing the file and handing it back to Luiz. "Where do we stand?"

Agent Wallace cleared his throat. "The search is ongoing. Four days now."

"Any new evidence or leads?"

He shook his head. "None. Boats are out trolling the lake, and, of course, we have divers in the water conducting circular and jackstay searches. Nothing found yet."

"When will we arrive at the lodge?" Chimalis asked.

"Tonight. That'll give us some cover as far as the media is concerned. They've got reporters from Anchorage staked out all over the place down there—CNN, MSNBC, Fox News. The fact that we haven't found a body yet is starting to 'raise eyebrows' as the media is often fond of saying when trying to bolster ratings. And of course, Senator Cooke's office has strongly encouraged us to conduct our investigation in secrecy. In fact, he's asked that, if we're ever confronted by the media, we state that we're part of the recovery operation and nothing more."

Chimalis shook her head. *Good luck trying to keep this a secret for long.* If the girl had been from a normal Alaskan family, perhaps they'd be able to keep it under wraps. For a senator's daughter? No chance. "You haven't set up a Joint Information Center yet to keep the media held in one location?"

Wallace chuckled, shook his head. "As I said, Agent Burton, we're a small operation. The local authority doesn't seem to really care about that."

She huffed in agitation and rubbed her forehead. "We're going to need a JIC if we're to do our job correctly *and* privately." She motioned to Luiz. "Will you see to that, Agent Vasquez?"

Luiz nodded. "Right away."

As Luiz was making the proper contacts via his cell phone, Chimalis paused a moment to collect her thoughts. She gazed out the window at the rolling forests of white spruce and birch trees that lined the road. The spruce was thick and green, with splotches of snow and ice. The white bark of the birch looked like snow, but Chimalis knew that that was an illusion. She wondered if what the senator's security official had seen was an illusion as well. Did he really see something pull the girl under the ice, or because of the distance and the inclement weather, had his eyes been tricked? Four days of searching had yielded nothing. Chimalis did not know how deep Kenai Lake was but she would expect that to be more than enough time to find the girl if such a creature hadn't abducted her.

She turned to Agent Wallace. "I requested dossiers on Inuit cryptids. Do you have them?"

"Yes," Wallace said, reaching into his satchel and pulling out a thick folder overflowing with documents. "This is what we were able to discover after talking with local Iñupiat leaders and elders. Each cryptid has its own stat sheet."

Chimalis took the folder and laid it over her lap. She counted through the paper-clipped bundles. Several different creatures. The Akhult, a combination of wolf and whale. She blanched. *Please, God, no more wolves!* She'd had enough of them for a while. The Tornit, a race of wild men much like Bigfoot. She shook her head. *Doesn't fit the situation.* An A-Mi-Kuk, a big, slimy creature infamous for burrowing underground and emerging in inland lakes. Chimalis nodded, raised a brow. Perhaps, though its physical description didn't fit the one that Cooke's security officer had put on closed record. Another and another and another. None of these cryptids fit the bill.

She reached the last one. She smiled and turned the pages around for her partner to see.

"This one, Luiz." Chimalis could hardly contain her relief at finally getting some actionable information. "This could be the one we're after."

⤫

NEAR DRIFTERS LODGE

The sweet energy from the girl was fading. Nipi could still feel the tingling warmth of the youthful essence course through her old veins, but it was no longer as sharp and energizing as when she had performed her first feeding. That had only been two days ago, and Nipi already felt hungry again.

She was grateful for Drifters Lodge. Far up Kenai Lake, away from the probing nuisance of divers trying to find her near Riverside, this lodge always had a number of children from which she could choose. Not as many girls this time as she had seen in the past, but what did that matter? Boys were just as useful as girls in their own way. Their energy was different: inherently more aggressive, more fitful. Sometimes, they died quickly. Sometimes, they lasted for months. Very unpredictable. But the three boys that she watched now, playing near the bank of the Kenai, gave her hope. They were quick, strong, vital. Especially the boy skipping rocks.

Nipi pressed her head through the thin layer of ice. She pushed up through the opening and into a small clump of drifted snow so that the boys would not see her. The rocks that the boy tossed skipped past her snow-covered head, just missing her by inches. She heard the clap of the rocks and their subtle vibrations along the ice sheet as they passed. The vibrations had a rhythm to them. Unsophisticated, unrefined, but Nipi liked it. She sang along with the skips.

This time, she pretended that she was a young throat singer, answering every musical phrase barked at her by a partner whose face lingered mere inches from her own. Back and forth, back and forth. As the rocks skipped by, she answered each vibration with a sheer note: skip…*da-da*, skip…*daoo*, skip… *alooala*, skip… again and again. The boys finally heard the notes.

"What is that?" she heard one of them ask. "Where's it coming from?"

"Don't know," another answered, and she replied to his non-committal response with a series of low, droning moans that scared them all. All, save for the boy skipping the rocks.

Finally, a rock struck her head. A splash of snow dropped from her face. The boy pointed. "What's that?"

"Beats me," another boy said. "A seal?"

The rock thrower shrugged. "Naw… it ain't moving."

I'm your friend.

One of the boys grew still, quiet. He reached over to the one closest to him, pushed him on the shoulder. "Come on… let's go back. My mom's coming home soon anyway."

They didn't wait or argue or concern themselves with the object that they had just struck with a rock. They gathered themselves up and climbed the bank toward the lodge. All but the boy who had skipped the rocks.

He lingered for several seconds. Then, he turned and looked out again at the snow-covered object he had struck.

Nipi smiled and let her throat music disappear in the cold wind. *Goodbye… we will sing again.*

As the boy scampered up the bank, Nipi slipped beneath the water.

CHAPTER FOUR

RIVERSIDE LODGE, ALASKA

They arrived at the lodge around 8PM, under a cloak of darkness and light snow. Both Chimalis and Luiz entered the lodge through a designated access point free from media entanglements. This being the case, Chimalis decided to take an evening stroll along the bank of the Kenai. Here at Riverside Lodge, the Kenai was more of a river, a narrow waterway that opened into the larger part of the lake further downstream. Carrying a flashlight, wearing relatively warm clothing, and with her dagger sheathed to her belt, she wandered along the riverbank. Further out into the river two FBI trolling boats searched for Elisapie's body. Chimalis shivered as she looked out toward the searchlights on the boats, and she hoped that she would *never* have to get on a boat for this mission.

She found a lot of shoe and boot prints from, she assumed, FBI agents and the swarming media. She also found some small footprints from the victim at the point where she had supposedly wandered out onto the ice. All of these locations were cordoned off, and none of them showed any footprints of any creature whatsoever. She hoped, of course, to stumble upon something more substantial, something the other agents had missed but, in truth, her real purpose for coming out here in the darkness was to just take a moment to decompress, to breathe in the cold air, to hear the slap of water along the riverbank, to take a moment to just get her bearings. She hoped, too, that perhaps she'd get a premonition or a feeling of some kind by just being near where the abduction had taken place and, of course, from the small piece of Elisapie's pajamas that Chimalis had removed from the girl's file and now held in her hand. Some VPA agents, like Apache shaman Joe Littlecloud, could sometimes get a feeling, a vision, just by being near a location where a cryptid event had occurred or by simply holding a piece of clothing from the victim. Chimalis had been lucky a couple of times with that, but not here, not now. Perhaps because the area was so foreign to her. Perhaps because it was so cold. Whatever the reason, she got nothing, save for a few moments to calm her nerves.

Returning to the lodge, she grabbed a bite to eat before taking a quick shower, then slept for a few hours. The next morning, the media was everywhere, despite Luiz having established a JIC about a half mile from the lodge.

"Sir," Chimalis said, putting up her hand to try to calm her growing anger. "Please step away from the riverbank. Your presence interferes with an official FBI investigation."

"An official VPA investigation, isn't that so?" asked the persistent journalist who was pushing against Luiz to try to get to Chimalis. "You're Special Agent Chimalis Burton, correct? One of the best Native American paranormal investigators in the United States. Your presence here clearly suggests that this case isn't just a drowning accident. It's something far, far more. What can you tell us about your mission here, Agent Burton?"

Chimalis shook her head. "I'm here as part of the recovery operation, sir. Nothing more."

"Does Senator Cooke know that you are here? Did he ask the VPA to investigate?"

Chimalis had had enough. "Sir, return to the JIC or I'll have you arrested. Luiz… escort him to the JIC… now!"

Luiz pushed the intransigent reporter back up the embankment as other FBI agents came down to assist. Chimalis turned away and tried to ignore the invasive questioning the journalist continued to throw at her as he was handled.

It's not a secret anymore, Senator, Chimalis thought as she shook her head, regained her composure, and surveyed the shoreline. *How could you think it ever would be?*

The light of day did not yield any further information. She did, however, get a better sense of area, the width of the river here at Riverside Lodge, the openness of the sky. Those things mattered, because it gave her some sense of the kind of creature that could function and thrive in this environment. The cryptid they sought was clearly a water creature. From the dossier she'd been provided, it was hard to know if the cryptid she suspected ever came ashore. Some aquatics did, some didn't. Again, no tracks had been discovered on the shoreline.

"Chimalis."

She started and turned. Luiz stood there beside a tall, thick man in a security uniform. Chimalis recognized him from his photo in the case dossier.

Luiz pointed to the man. "This is Victor Rowland. He is the security officer that reported the abduction of Elisapie Cooke."

Chimalis extended a hand. Victor took it and shook it slowly. "Agent Burton," he said. "Thank you for coming."

She nodded. "Mr. Rowland, I've read your statement on the abduction, but if you could just walk us through the event, moment by moment, that would be most helpful."

Victor nodded. He paused to get his bearings and to survey the grounds. He looked up the embankment, back to the river, and then walked left along the water's edge for about thirty feet. He stopped. He pointed to the ground where there were several small boot prints. "Elisapie stood here when I first noticed her.

"I was in the kitchen. Me and another security guard. We were having coffee, talking a little. We didn't hear Elisapie come out of her room." He bowed his head, sighed. "I guess we should have. I did hear the front door rattle a little. But it did that anyway; it was a little loose. So, I didn't think much of it.

"A little while later, I happened to glance out the kitchen window." Victor pointed again to the ground. "And she was here, right here. And then I saw her step out onto the ice."

"How far did she step out, Mr. Rowland?" Chimalis asked.

He shook his head, shrugged. "About ten feet. Maybe twelve. As soon as I saw her through the window, I jumped up and took off after her. By the time I got down to the embankment, she was already on the ice. I pulled my pistol..." he pulled it now from his holster and aimed it out to the water, "...and aimed it at the creature. I fired and —"

"That was a risky thing to do, sir," Chimalis said. "You could have hit the girl."

Victor seemed annoyed by the statement. "I'm an excellent shot, Agent Burton. I only aimed it. I didn't fire. Not at first, anyway. I called out to Elisapie. I threatened to fire if the creature — or whatever it was — didn't let go."

"Then you fired?" Luiz asked.

Victor nodded, tucking the pistol back into its holster. "I did. Two shots above their heads. I would never risk shooting Elisapie."

"And the shots did not deter or frighten the creature?"

"No. I called to Elisapie once more, but the beast pulled her under."

The man seemed to be on the verge of tears. Chimalis sympathized, but time was running out. She could not afford to give this man time to calm himself. "Can you describe the creature for me, sir?"

He sniffled and collected himself, then said, "A thin woman."

"A woman? Are you certain?"

He nodded. "Yes. Not really a fully human face, like yours, for example, but smoother. Like a fish face. Not scaly, but green with a hint of grey, like it had veins running across its face pumping grey blood. I couldn't tell what kind of teeth it had, but it was a woman's figure. Thin, lanky. It had on a parka, but its hair was dark, long, like coils of braided rope. It was a woman, all right. I'm certain of that."

"Did it bite the girl?" Chimalis asked. "Was it choking her as she was pulled under the ice?"

Victor looked to the sky, deep in thought. He squinted, said, "No, not that I recall. It seemed… careful with her, you know? Like it was trying to cradle her and put her in a pouch on the back of her parka." Surprisingly, he smiled. "And I heard music, like someone was singing in the distance."

"Singing?" Chimalis took a step closer to the man. "You did not mention anything in your statement about singing."

He seemed surprised, as if Chimalis wasn't being truthful. "I didn't? Hm. I thought I had. Yeah, singing. Just for a moment, and then it was gone. As soon as Elisapie disappeared underneath the ice, the singing stopped."

Chimalis put her face to the breeze, hoping to hear some of that reported music. Nothing, of course, save for the music of nature, which to her, despite the cold temperatures and unfamiliar surroundings, was quite pleasant. She made a mental note to consider coming back here some time on vacation… when the weather was warmer, when the place wasn't swarming with Search and Rescue crews.

"Once the girl was pulled beneath the ice," Chimalis asked, "did you make any attempt to try to retrieve her?"

Victor cast his eyes down to the soft ground again, seemingly despondent at her question. "No. I wanted to. I made steps toward the bank, I fired a couple more shots, but my instincts told me to call the authorities. I pulled out my phone and did that instead."

"Which was probably the wise choice, Mr. Rowland." Chimalis came up beside him and put her hand on his shoulder. "You did the right thing. Had you tried to enter the water, the creature might have taken you as well."

He shook his head. "It doesn't feel like the wise choice."

Chimalis smiled. "Thank you, Mr. Rowland. I may have questions for you later, but you may go now."

He bid them farewell and climbed up the bank. Chimalis watched him go, then turned toward the river.

"What you thinking, boss?" Luiz asked.

She shook her head, said nothing. She watched the water, under a thin, cracking sheet of ice, slap against the bank. She put out her foot and took a step into the thick icy muck. Her anxiety spiked as memories from her past flooded back into her mind, memories of water mixed with blood. Distant memories; terrifying memories.

"I would not take another step if I were you, Chimalis Burton."

Both Chimalis and Luiz turned toward the voice. An old woman stood along the edge of the embankment.

"There's an old Inuit Proverb," the old woman said. "'You never really know your friends from your enemies... until the ice breaks.'"

"Who are you?" Chimalis asked, stepping away from the bank and toward Luiz. She had a notion to pull her pistol. Luiz looked to do the same. Chimalis put her hand on Luiz's arm to keep him still. "If you are a reporter, whoever you are, you need to go to the JIC and—"

"I'm not a reporter, Chimalis Burton," the woman said, stepping away from the embankment and moving closer. She put up her hands in supplication. They were old, cracked, withered. "Nor am I someone that you and your companion should fear. I am here to help you find the creature you seek."

Chapter Five

Bored, bored, bored!

It was not uncommon for Toklo to feel this way. Nearing the end of winter and having been cooped up in the cabin all these long months, watching the same old cartoons and old Westerns, while his mother and father worked various maintenance jobs around the lodge. A couple of boys from Anchorage had stayed over the weekend. He had some fun playing with them, but they were gone now. Snow was falling, and Toklo was bored.

He clicked through the usual channels on their flat-screen TV, found a couple streaming cartoons that appealed to his interests, but didn't linger there for long. He looked out the frosted window. Beautiful, beautiful snow falling everywhere. Toklo smiled. He wanted to go outside.

"Don't go near the lake," his mother had told him. "While we are working, you stay near the cabin."

News on the TV had said that a senator's daughter had fallen through the ice and had drowned. Mother and Father had spoken about the event in whispers beyond Toklo's hearing, but from what he could figure out, they didn't believe the news. Something else had happened to the girl; what, Toklo did not know. *Inuit intuition,* his grandmother would call it. There was something about the details of the event that his parents didn't believe; something was wrong. *Don't go near the lake...* Toklo would listen to that warning.

But they didn't tell him not to go outside.

Toklo flicked off the TV, put on cold-weather gear, and stepped out into the falling snow.

A light snow, one that Toklo could brush off his coat if necessary. It wasn't very cold either, which was good. A perfect day to do... what, exactly? He wasn't sure, but it wasn't warm enough to pack snow and make a snowman or a castle of some kind. Instead, he decided to just kick the snow around, make a path around their cabin, like a moat that Toklo had seen in history books at school. Their cabin certainly wasn't a castle, but perhaps he could pretend it was. For a little while, anyway.

He was a knight, high stepping through the snow, kicking it up into his walking path. The wind blew it back on his face, into his mouth. Toklo let the snow melt on his tongue and felt cold tingles on his cheeks. He thought about brushing the snow away, but decided to leave it alone. Such important work he was doing protecting their "castle" from the evils of the world. He did not have time to pause and cleanse himself. Besides, it wasn't that cold.

Toklo whistled while he marched. Short, staccato beats, high-pitched, drifting into the wind and disappearing almost instantly. The whistles kept his pace, and so he kept whistling even though snow still drifted onto his face.

Somewhere in the distance a woman's voice answered his whistles. It sounded distant to Toklo, anyway. First, she whistled too, like him, though lower. It matched his song beat for beat. He changed his tune, a higher pitch, and she matched it, tone for tone. He changed again; she matched him. Over and over, like their faces were close to each other, trading notes back and forth, like Inuit girls do when throat singing.

Toklo paused a few feet from completing his moat and enclosing his cabin in a protective cocoon. He wanted to finish his work, but her voice, her music, was too mesmerizing, too intoxicating as his father might say, for him to go on. Toklo loved her voice, and he had to find her.

He stepped out of his neatly cut path and went to the front of the cabin. He paused so that he could listen to her music and tell where it was coming from. Silence, save for the rustle of wind, the light sprinkle of snow still falling.

"There it is," he said out loud with a smile, not realizing at first that he had done so. "There it is."

He turned to face the lake shore. The music wasn't coming from the water, or from across the lake. No. It came from a pile of snow near the shore.

Toklo found that odd. Not the music, but the large pile. It wasn't snowing very hard, and the wind wasn't blowing strongly. Yet there it was, taller than he, tapered at the top like an icicle, or one of those anthills from Africa that he had seen on the Science Channel. A tall white pillar, like a tree stump, but one with music rolling out of its fluffy center like a waterfall. And, it had a smell also. That, too, was odd. Since when did sound have smell? But Toklo could smell it, and it reminded him of roasting seal meat, the kind he had tasted when Mom and Dad had taken him to the Great Northern Arts Festival a few years ago. A wonderful smell that made his mouth water. Toklo smiled. He took a step forward. *Don't go near the lake...* His mother's warning rang clear in his ear. He shrugged it off. *I won't be going to the lake, Mama. The music isn't coming from there.*

It was coming from the snow pile. So, Toklo walked to it, slowly, cautiously, for fear of slipping, for the ground to the pile sloped downward. He had slipped before and had bruised his bottom, as his mother called it. He and his friends called it an 'ass,' like normal people did. He did not want that to happen again, and then, what would he tell Mother once she and Father got home? He walked slowly to the snow pile, stopping in front of it.

The snow pile rustled, shimmied as if hit by an earthquake. Light snow cascaded down to the base, and a face appeared.

It's that thing on the lake the other day that I hit with a rock. But now it had a *real* face. Light green, flat, like that of a fish, yet clearly a woman, for there she stood, taller than he, thin, frail, as if the wind could blow her away with the snow.

Come to me... Her voice lilted upward, high-pitched, but oh so lovely. *Come to me, Toklo, and come* with *me...*

He stepped forward, overcome by her music. So soothing and inviting, like his mother's voice when she used to sing to him as a baby. *Come with me, Toklo. Come...*

"Come?" He was up against the snow pile now, his face close to hers. "Come where?"

On an adventure...

Toklo tried to speak, but her arms came out of the snow like hammers punching a press. She grabbed him, and she was stronger than she looked. Her arms were nothing but old, withered flesh and brittle bone. But, she held him tightly as he screamed and tried to get away. Toklo punched her in the face, and that seemed to shock her. But she held on, her long, black claws cutting through his coat. Now, her voice dropped low, feral, as if she growled. And yet, she held on.

Toklo screamed again, this time for his mother. But, she did not answer, so far away from the cabin, so far away from her and Father.

Working somewhere many cabins away, too far away to hear his screaming. He tried to punch the woman in the face again, but she wrapped a leather pouch over his head. She wrapped it tightly and he fell into it as if he were a baby kangaroo, falling and falling, as if he were small again, and his mother held him against her breast nursing. Toklo struggled to break free from the pouch, but the woman snarled at him through the bag, then hoisted it up onto her back like he was nothing but a pile of dirty laundry.

The music returned, her soft, soothing voice speaking to him through the leather pouch, telling him to be calm, relax, and that everything would be all right.

And it would be. Toklo was convinced of that now, for her voice told him so. It told him that everything would be okay, that he would be safe in her company. They were going on a grand adventure, just the two of them, and he was happy to do so.

Toklo calmed. Closing his eyes, he fell asleep.

Chapter Six

Her name was Sakari Kolit. She wore what Chimalis assumed was traditional Inuit clothing: coveralls of soft caribou skin with a thick, furry parka thrown over her shoulders, covering her arms and chest. Mittens were tied at her waist. Her boots were sealskin tan. Her hair hung long and grey. She had an elaborate tattoo across her forehead and down onto her right cheek. She carried no weapons; Luiz made sure of that.

"I'm sure you have knowledge about the creature you seek, Ms. Burton," Sakari said as they all sat in the cabin established as the headquarters for the VPA operation. "But, if you'll indulge me, I will describe it for you, far better than any report or book will do."

Chimalis had to stop herself from blurting out that she had little to no good information about the creature, other than the data the Anchorage FBI agent had provided, which was useful, but it was always best to hear it from someone close to the culture from which the cryptid evolved. It did not seem likely that this woman was lying. Everything about her spoke of authenticity.

Chimalis nodded. "Please continue, Ms. Kolit."

"Call me Sakari. I do not require a formal address." She cleared her throat and stood before them, holding her arms out as if she were on display. "I am wearing a parka, an *amautik* as it is known among the Inuit. It has a pouch for children, for babies." She tugged on it hard. "This is what the creature uses to kidnap children.

"It is called a Qallupilluk, or Qalupalik, or Qallupilluit… there are many pronunciations. That doesn't matter. What matters most, Chimalis Burton, is that it's a killer. It is like a siren from ancient Greek mythology, only worse. It does not feed on adult men, mariners who hear its song and dash their boats upon the rocks. No. The Qalupalik kidnaps and kills children. It feeds on them to draw out their youthful energies, their vitality, so that it can live, hopefully, forever."

Chimalis leaned forward. "You've seen this creature?"

Sakari nodded and took a seat. "Yes. But, like its name, its physical descriptions vary. Some say that it has fins like a fish, with green scaly skin and a flat face. Some say that its skin is grey and smooth. Some say its limbs are long, lanky, bony. Others say it shifts from emaciation to puffiness, depending upon its feeding cycle. Some say its teeth and claws are black and sharp. Some say its eyes are dark, deep, soulless.

"But I tell you truthfully, Chimalis Burton, that the one you seek is more woman than fish, though its skin *is* sallow green with hints of grey. It does not have scales or fins. Its hair is dark, long, luxurious. Its claws are black and sharp. Its teeth are jagged and chipped, like an old woman's might be. And, it is relentless. It will abduct another child… and soon."

Chimalis waited until Sakari had removed her parka and set it on the nearby table. She was sweating, and was that a hint of a tear lining the bottom of her right eye? She did not want to ask the next question, but she had to. "And, how do you know so much about this Qalupalik, Sakari?"

The tear fell, marking a wet line down Sakari's face. The woman wiped it away, sniffled, and continued. "My sister was taken by this monster. Sixty years ago, when I was ten and she seven."

Chimalis could tell that Sakari's memory of her sister was painful, but she said nothing. In her official capacity as a VPA agent, she could not allow her own emotions to supersede the investigation.

Chimalis almost laughed out loud at that.

There had been many times during her career that she had succumbed to her emotions during a case. How could one not succumb when supernatural elements, like *El Cadejo*, could penetrate your mind, your thoughts and emotions, and fill you with dread, hate, anger, fear, you name it. But, not here, not now. Chimalis needed information, and for that, she needed to remain calm, detached, and dispassionate. For now, at least.

Chimalis took a pen and pad of paper off the table and began scribbling notes. "Can you describe for me your sister's abduction?"

A pause, another sniffle, then, "Lusa and I were throat singers. My mother insisted that we be so. We didn't mind. In fact, we loved singing. We would practice near the shoreline of the Yukon River.

That's where we lived. In the early spring, a lot of driftwood would float down the river and pile up by our village, and we would stand alongside the wood and sing." She giggled. "Sing about driftwood and other silly, nonsensical things like dancing fish and sea lions and mud, singing whales, and whatever else we wanted to sing about. Back and forth, back and forth. We were good.

"Mother warned us about getting too close to the river. 'A Qalupalik will get you,' she would say, wagging her finger at us. But, you know, we were children, unaware, believing that it was nothing more than a silly myth, something that parents told their children to keep them away from strong, flowing rivers or thin, dangerous ice along a bank. In our minds, the Qalupalik wasn't real. So, when Mother went to the market, Lusa and I would go to the riverbank and sing. Sing, sing, sing all morning long."

Sakari's tone suddenly turned serious. Her smile disappeared. "One morning, we heard a voice through a pile of driftwood. More like a humming and a tap, tap, tap. We ignored it at first, thinking that the tapping was a Downy Woodpecker or a sapsucker or some other bird. The humming we thought was an echo of our own voices. But, it persisted, and eventually, the humming fell in chorus to our own songs." She shook her head. "Inuit throat music, Chimalis Burton, is not the work of a trio.

"Lusa, ever the curious one, crawled over the driftwood to have a look. I wasn't sure if she should do it, but the wood pile wasn't too close to the river, and I too was curious. So, she crawled over it, slowly, whistling as she went. She was trying to mimic a bird's whistle, to see if she could spook whatever it was out of the drift.

"Then, the humming stopped, and in its place, music. The most beautiful voice I had ever heard. I've been a voice coach most of my life; I know a beautiful voice when I hear one. I too was nearly mesmerized by the tones, the shifting from head voice to chest voice, the way that the singer so skillfully used diphthongs to accentuate vowels and syllables. I know Lusa was mesmerized as well. She kept crawling over that driftwood toward that voice, and I almost found myself cheering her on.

"Then, the wood cracked, like someone had grabbed it and snapped it in two. This creature, hair long and dark, arms long, skin green and grey, reached out from underneath the wood and snatched Lusa, so damn quickly I didn't react. I couldn't move. I wasn't sure exactly what was going on, the music still cloudy and sweet in my mind. Then, Lusa screamed, and I jumped toward her, screaming myself. I tried grabbing her feet, her legs. The Qalupalik stared me straight in the face, hissing and howling, and then ran a long, black claw over my forearm."

Sakari rolled up her right sleeve to reveal the thick red scar. Chimalis leaned forward again to get a good look. She shook her head. *Terrible.*

The old woman pushed her sleeve down and continued. "I managed to grab hold of Lusa's foot, but the monster was too strong, and I was just a child. I lost my sister that day, Chimalis Burton. Do you know what it feels like to lose a sibling?"

Being an only child, Chimalis had no frame of reference. Luiz spoke up, "I lost my brother to cancer when he was twelve."

Sakari looked at Luiz and nodded. "Then you understand. Three months later, Lusa's body was found alongside the Yukon River." She wiped away another tear. "She was nothing more than a husk. A dried-up piece of driftwood, just skin and bones."

Sakari stood, grabbed her parka, and put it back on. "From that day, Chimalis Burton, I vowed to find this beast and kill it. I have not been successful, obviously, for the Qalupalik roams all the northern waters, from Alaska to Russia, to Iceland, Greenland, and Northern Europe. It had been gone a long, long time. But now it is back... and I intend on seeing it destroyed."

Chimalis finished writing a few notes. She put the pen and pad down and said with a sigh, "You understand, Ms. Kolit, that this Qalupalik may not be the one that took your sister. It's my understanding that there are more than one of these cryptids in the world."

Sakari shook her head. "No, I'm certain this is the one."

"How can you be sure?"

"I just know it, Chimalis Burton. When you watch your sister being taken by such a brute, and you look into its eyes, and it cuts you to the bone with its long claw, you know... you know."

Luiz cleared his throat, asked, "How is it possible, Ms. Kolit, for this Qalupalik to keep these children alive for so long, to feed on their 'youthful energies'?"

"She must keep them alive through some form of magic," Chimalis offered. She'd seen it before. Many cryptids had such abilities. But, keeping someone under such a spell for so long... *a powerful creature, indeed.*

"You have three months to find Senator Cooke's daughter," Sakari said. "Three months before she too is found dried up like a husk on a bank somewhere. Like my sister."

Stinging words, Chimalis had to admit, but truthful ones, if what the woman was saying were true.

Three months…

Agent Wallace didn't bother knocking. He burst through the door.

"We're in the middle of an interview here, Agent Wallace," Chimalis said. "Please, will you wait outside until—"

"My apologies, Agent Burton," he said, handing her a note, "but we've got a problem."

Chimalis took the note, read it silently. Sighing, she crumpled it up and tossed it onto the table. "Another child has gone missing at Drifters Lodge. This time, a boy."

Silence in the room. Chimalis looked up at Sakari. The old woman huffed and winked sarcastically. "Now, you have two children to find in three months."

Chapter Seven

The situation didn't feel right to Chimalis. Sakari had said that the Qalupalik could feed for at least three months on its victim. Why, then, had it snatched another, and relatively close to the first abduction? What purpose did that serve other than to draw unwarranted attention to it as it moved downstream toward Kenai Lake proper? Why?

The parents of the young boy who had gone missing were frantic. Sakari consoled them while Chimalis and Luiz canvassed the area around their cabin. "This is pissing me off, Luiz," Chimalis said as she walked around the cabin in a path through the snow that, perhaps, the boy, Toklo, had created before his abduction. "Two abductions in less than a week. And children. Nothing pisses me off more than cryptids that target kids. We've got to put an end to this shit, and soon."

Chimalis reflexively reached for the knife at her waist. It felt comforting to know that it was there, intact, and ready. She felt for her pistol as well. Good that it was there also.

She reached the end of the path that Toklo had created. It had ended abruptly, the circle incomplete. Chimalis halted and looked towards the shoreline. She craned her ear to the breeze. No singing, no music save for chirping birds. The Qalupalik was gone.

They found a snowdrift with several footprints around its base, and not just Toklo's. Chimalis smiled and pointed. "Look here, Luiz. Crazy bitch risked coming ashore to nab the boy."

The Qalupalik's print showed a long, thin foot. Practically human, though the claw marks, with tiny droplets of frozen blood, made it clear what it was: a killer. Chimalis followed the path from the snowdrift to the shoreline. "It pulled the boy from the drift and entered the river here. Damn! Where the hell did it go?"

Luiz shrugged. "Probably back to where it has stashed the girl."

"Where is that? Upstream? Down? Nearby?"

"I don't know, boss, but we need to get some boats out on the river and do a sonar search. See if we can find a cave or something."

Chimalis nodded. "Indeed, and we need to set a trap for it as well." She tapped him on the shoulder. "Come, let's take a look at your map."

Toklo's parents allowed them to use their kitchen table to lay out Luiz's map of the Kenai Lake area, from Riverside Lodge down to the Primrose Campgrounds, where the lake again became a river. With a red pen, Chimalis circled Riverside and Drifters Lodge, then ran her finger down the river from the location of the first abduction to the second. "Two miles apart, roughly." She shook her head. "Doesn't it seem odd to you that this Qalupalik would attack again so quickly, and so close together?"

"It does indeed, boss. But Ms. Kolit did say that it would not stop doing so."

Chimalis nodded. "Yes, and she said a lot of other things, too. Would you please call her in here?"

Luiz left the room. Chimalis continued moving her finger down the river until she reached Kenai Lake proper. From there on down to Primrose, there were a few other campsites, lodges, but not many. As requested, Luiz had investigated and penciled in those locations where children were most likely to be. Now with this second abduction, it was very likely that families with any children living or vacationing near Kenai Lake would be removed. Which meant one thing to Chimalis: the Qalupalik would attack again, and soon. Was it even aware that it was being investigated? Did it even care? And, again, why was it being so reckless as to continue to abduct children along a lake that was, for all intense and purposes, not a very large body of water?

One thing Chimalis had learned in her years of researching and vanquishing cryptids was that they were, for the most part, animals, and animals worked on instinct. Without doubt, this Qalupalik was a creature of habit. It would continue its destructive path down the river toward Primrose.

Luiz and Sakari entered the room. Chimalis nodded. "Thank you, Sakari, for giving comfort to Toklo's parents."

The old woman bowed slightly. "It's the least I can do, knowing well the pain that comes with losing a loved one to this *beast*."

"It's confirmed that the boy was abducted by the Qalupalik. Luiz and I found evidence near the riverside. We must move quickly, now, if we want to get ahead of this creature. Here's what I want to do." Chimalis smoothed out the map and pointed to two locations. "Based on this map, here are the two most likely campsites where it may strike again: Camp K—or Cooper's Landing—and Quartz Creek. There are employees and campers there with children, and they are unlikely to leave these locations now that spring is coming on and more tourists and vacationers will be arriving within the next few weeks. I'll go to Camp K. Luiz will go to Quartz Creek. We will hole up at these locations and wait for her to arrive.

"We'll also begin a full sonar sweep of the river and lake. Alaskan resources for VPA work are meager, but I'm sure Senator Cooke will approve, and perhaps pay for, any additional resources we require."

Chimalis waited to see if Sakari would say something, give any hint of approval or disagreement with the plan. Finally, she said, "And what will you ask of me, Chimalis Burton? I'm at your service. Where shall I assist?"

"You will be with me," Chimalis said. "And there is one other thing I would like you to tell me, Ms. Kolit."

"Yes?"

Chimalis smiled. "The truth."

"I'm sorry?"

"Ms. Kolit… Sakari. You stated, rather definitively, that you believed that this Qalupalik would abduct another child very soon. You then made the conflicting statement that it can feed on a child for three months. Why, then, has it abducted another so soon after the first? If it can feed for three months on just one, why did it so quickly take another and risk exposing itself a second time? You know something more about this creature that you haven't shared." Chimalis stepped forward, her eyes fixed on the old woman's drawn and worried face. "What are you not telling me, Sakari?"

The old woman cast her eyes down to her soft boots. She fidgeted, seemed agitated, worried. It was clear that she did not want to say anything further, but Chimalis held her ground, waited, and did not waver on her demand.

Finally, Sakari sighed, then said, "I did not want to confess this because I haven't even told my own family, Chimalis Burton. But… yes. There is something I didn't tell you.

"Like me, the Qalupalik is dying."

Chapter Eight

Three hundred years old. Yes, that's my age!

How stupid that she couldn't remember her own age before, but Nipi now literally glowed in the energies that these two children gave her: one hand on the girl's face; one on the boy's. A perfect combination. All her memories, her knowledge, came flooding back. She looked at her arms, hands. They, too, plumped with youthful, powerful vitality. She was a young woman again, alert, capable of anything.

And yet, the children. The boy seemed withered and frail with only one touch, one feeding. The girl—Elisapie?—had shrunk to mouse size. Not literally, of course, but she seemed to have dropped several pounds after just two feedings. Her breathing was sound; the spell Nipi had cast upon her held. Toklo's as well. That was a comfort, but their bodies were changing, and so quickly. *Why is this happening?* Nipi wondered. *Why?*

Fifty years ago, she could have gone for months feeding on only one child. Now... how much time did she have? Two weeks? Three? A month?

She quickly pulled her hands away from their faces, the cold, dirty water swirling madly around their bodies. Nipi looked at them and smiled. So angelic they seemed, even the boy, in quiet, sleepy repose. It was almost terrible to think about how they might look in just a few days. *Perhaps I should let them go?*

She had released a few in her life: children whom she had abducted but, for one reason or another, could not satisfy her hunger. Most of them had had diseases of some kind, terminal illnesses that, with one feeding, were apparent. To Nipi, they had tasted like sour milk. And there were others that she had considered letting go: a boy near Nuuk, Greenland, that had begged and pleaded so strongly that, for a moment, she felt guilty about taking him. The girl at Point Hope, Alaska, whose furry white Malamute howled so terribly as she was being pulled under the water. The driftwood girl on the Yukon River whose sister almost killed herself trying to save her sibling.

These two? No. As sweet as they were, lying there before her, Nipi could not risk releasing them. How would she feed, survive without then? *Am I dying?* She scowled and hissed at the notion. *No, never. I cannot die!*

But she needed at least one more. One more child would do it. Then, she could sip from each of them, a little at a time, and draw out their lives for many months. *Yes… one more.*

Nipi ran her plump fingers across Elisapie's and Toklo's tender cheeks, and then, she left the cave.

She knew where she would go, where she would find a third child. She had drifted past the place on her way to Riverside. She had seen many children playing there by the shoreline. A dog or two as well, which might be a risk, but so be it. They would not stop her from doing what she needed to do, what her instincts demanded that she do.

A third child would make all the difference.

Chapter Nine

"I have cancer," Sakari said as she and Chimalis and a handful of other FBI agents made their way down Kenai Lake toward Camp K, the most logical place for the Qalupalik to attack because, according to the record, Camp K was often called the "children's camp." Chimalis sat at the center of the boat, white-knuckle gripping the arm rests of her chair, trying desperately not to vomit.

"It's terminal," Sakari continued as she leaned against the railing of the craft, trying to stay out of the way of the agents scrambling around the deck. "I didn't want to say anything because dying is a personal matter, Chimalis Burton. I haven't told my family. I felt that they should know first before anyone else. But I do apologize for not having told you my suspicion about the Qalup—are you all right?"

No, dammit, I'm not! The words were on the tip of her lips. She wanted to blurt them out, but doing so would not allay her fear and anxiety of the water splashing against their moving boat and the old, terrible images in her mind. "I'm fine. Please, continue."

Sakari cleared her throat. "I believe the Qalupalik is dying because she would never come this far inland to search for children; moving along the shoreline of the ocean is more productive and safer for her. And she would never attack again so quickly after her first victim. She needs more children because she needs more energy."

Chimalis cleared her throat, swallowing back the big lump that had churned up from her queasy stomach. "Then, that likely means we don't have three months to find these children. She'll use them up quickly."

The pressures of this mission, coupled with the burning sensation in her throat for being on this awful boat, gave Chimalis pause. *Perhaps it would be better just to let the thing die,* she thought. How long would that take, and how many other children would be abducted before it finally succumbed? Something "dying" could last many, many more months. No. It was foolish to even consider letting the matter run its course. Chimalis shook her head, swallowed again, and rubbed sweat from her brow. Sweat in thirty-degree weather. *Safe, solid ground can't come fast enough.*

They drew alongside the pier at Camp K and moored the boat. Chimalis was the first to disembark. She breathed a sigh of relief and turned back to the agents still on deck. "Start your sonar scan immediately and keep it hot. Any significant movement detected, you let me know."

"Yes, ma'am."

Chimalis walked up the pier. Sakari followed closely behind, quietly humming a tune. "What are you singing?" Chimalis asked.

"A prayer."

Chimalis smiled. "I appreciate your spiritual support, but I'll be fine. We'll be fine."

"I'm not singing for your safety, Chimalis Burton. I'm singing for Luiz's."

Quartz Creek

What is this thing *tied to the pier?*

It was a boat, of course, and Nipi knew that. But it was different. It emitted waves of sound, pulses that spread through the water and pierced her ears, threatening to drive her mad. She was blind, the sound waves so strong that she couldn't see or think, couldn't decide where to swim, how to get ashore and take a new child on an adventure.

The sound reached far into the water. Nipi tried to avoid it, to swim along the very edge of the sound waves, to ease closer to the pier so that she could hop out of the water and find the child on land. It was a risky thing to do. She could survive out of water, but only for a short time. She had gotten out of the water to take Toklo on an adventure, but the snow had drifted just at the right time, in the right spot; her skin could absorb the snow and stay fresh and clean. There was no snow now, and no rain. Still cold, and that was a comfort. Her green-grey skin, now plump and smooth from such good feedings, would wither, dry, and crack if she stayed out of the water for too long. But she had to try, had to risk it.

I need a third child!

She waited until the sound wave passed her. She refocused, regained her sight, and made for the stern of the boat. There, she found a ladder.

Nipi reached out of the water, grabbed the first rung, and pulled herself out of Kenai Lake.

The air was cold, frigid. It felt good. Nipi lingered on the ladder, hidden behind the stern from the voices echoing across the deck. It wasn't a large boat. Perhaps thirty, forty feet. The voices—three, maybe four—seemed serious, official. Nipi tried to understand what they were saying, but their words were too complex for her to decipher. A wave of sound rippled through the water below her, but it did not hurt her ears like before. She was out of the water and ready to hunt.

But first, these creatures on the boat. She let them talk for a few more seconds, and then she sang.

Nipi put all her energy, strength into singing the most beautiful song she could think of…

Still now, and hear my singing;
put away your troubles, and come to me…

She sang in Inuktitut, the language of many Inuit, those that she remembered the most from her youth. She doubted that these boat creatures would understand. That did not matter. What mattered was that they heard her voice and that they loved it. Who wouldn't? Nipi was the greatest singer ever. All children loved her voice.

These creatures on the boat were not children, and it was clear to her that what they were doing was a direct attempt to harm her. She could think of no other explanation for the sound waves in the water. *They are here to hurt me. To make me suffer. To keep me from feeding. I cannot let that happen.*

She sang the verse again, and again, and their incessant, non-sensical blather stopped. One of them said, "Do you hear that?"

"Yeah, what is that?"

"I don't know."

Nipi could hear them moving out of the cabin and toward the stern. She put all her newly consumed energy into singing, moving the words up and down all her registers, high then low, high and low again, like an angel. Like Sila, the Inuit god of the sky, of wind and weather. Her voice called them to the stern, and they listened.

"It's beautiful."

"Yeah… it is."

Still now, and hear my singing;
put away your troubles, and swim…

"It's such a beautiful night," one of them said, now close enough for Nipi to see the tips of her shoes. "Isn't it such a beautiful night?"

"Yes," another said, shuffling his feet closer and closer to the stern. He leaned over the railing. "A wonderful night for a swim."

Still now, and hear my singing;
put away your troubles, fall into the water,
and breathe, and breathe, and breathe…

One fell in, then another, and another, as Nipi kept firm the notes in her throat, singing them out until all three of the creatures were in the lake. Their heads disappeared below the water line, and Nipi kept singing until she could not feel their thrashing rivulets through the water. The last one opened his mouth, gulped in a lungful of the cold, mucky water, and fell silent.

Nipi stopped singing and climbed aboard the boat.

She was weaker now. The singing had pulled a lot of energy from her body. Gone again were the memories of her youth and the vitality that she had experienced then as a child herself, when she, like all the children she took on an adventure, had been lured to a frozen lake and taken by an old crone. *Am I the old crone now?* She wondered. She felt that way, walking across the deck toward the cabin of plexiglass windows and machines that flickered different colors and sounds. *Am I dying?*

Not if she got that third child. But first, she had to take care of this boat.

It wasn't just the three adult creatures that she had sent to their eternal rest; this boat was also a threat. Nipi stepped into the cabin. All quiet, save for a perpetual *bip-bip-bip* of a machine to her right, and the annoying flashing of another machine to her left. All the beeping and flashing, and now, a voice came through another machine… *"Luiz… Luiz… do you read? Come in, Luiz."*

No 'Luiz' responded, for no one was in the cabin but her. Was this 'Luiz' one of the creatures she had sent into the water? Probably so, and good riddance.

No further delay. Nipi ignored the woman's voice droning on about Luiz, stepped to the right, flashed her thick black claws, bared her jagged teeth, shrieked, then slashed the machine in half.

And another, and another, and another, until all that was left was nothing but a pile of destroyed equipment and torn, sparking electrical wires.

CAMP K, COOPER LANDING

"Dammit!"

Chimalis cursed so loudly that Sakari jumped. "What is wrong?"

"Communication has been severed."

"Why?"

Chimalis shook her head. "I don't know."

There were several plausible reasons why: they could be having problems with their equipment; the weather could be interfering; they could have all disembarked with Luiz to provide protection for his campsite interviews. Many reasons.

"What should we do?" Sakari asked.

"Nothing," Chimalis said stepping to the edge of the boat. "Probably just a malfunction. We'll keep trying."

There was nothing to worry about. The agents with Luiz were professionals, and Luiz was more than capable of handling the situation.

Chimalis stared into the cold, sloshing water. She felt a chill across her back. The moon was out, so the idea of weather being a factor for their communication problem was unlikely. It was equipment issues. Had to be.

Moonlight twinkled in the water. Chimalis shivered again as she stared into its depths. The light of the moon was pleasant, and it invited her to jump in. For a moment, Chimalis considered it, but how silly would that be? She—

The moonlight dancing across the water suddenly turned a deep blood red. It swirled up in a funnel, and through the funnel came an image, the face of an old friend. The blood streamed out of her friend's mouth and eyes like water from a hose.

The image changed. Now, the Qalupalik appeared, smiling, raising a hand, calling on Chimalis to jump in. Then Luiz, sweet, competent Luiz, smiling up at her as he always did. Over and over the faces changed, too fast for Chimalis to see them clearly. Then they stopped. It was just Luiz's face now, holding there on the surface, surround in a pool of bloody water, calling to her, his face contorted in an agonizing scowl. *Help me!*

Chimalis turned and walked to the agents trying to establish contact with Luiz. "Gun the engines. We need to get to Quartz Creek… now!"

QUARTZ CREEK

Luiz Vasquez thought he heard something, an echo of sound drifting from the shoreline, from the SAR boat from which he had disembarked, coming ashore to canvass the campground. He paused, took a listen, then continued. *Nothing to worry about,* he thought. Three very qualified agents were aboard, conducting extensive sonar sweeps of the lake, and keeping the boss up to speed on things. Luiz had chosen to mute his cell phone to focus on the matter at hand: ensuring that all civilians here at Quartz Creek were safe. So far, so good.

The campground was relatively large, but Luiz was grateful that few campers were present. Only eight RVs and a few tents constructed and occupied. Not many children, but there were some. He had already talked to half the visitors. Now, he stepped up to another RV and knocked lightly on the door. He waited. A hand pushed the door curtain aside. A soft, round, and pleasant face appeared through the window. "Yes?"

Luiz checked his occupancy list. He then flashed his FBI credentials. "Good evening, Ms. Waska? I'm Agent Luiz Vasquez. May I speak with you for a moment?"

She seemed reluctant at first. Luiz smiled and took a step back to give her room. Finally, she unlocked and opened the door. She stood in the gap, clearly not wanting this government official to come in. Luiz didn't press it.

"Good evening, Ms. Waska," he said again, tucking away his ID. "Thank you for taking time to speak with me. You are aware of the disappearance of Senator Cooke's daughter, yes?"

She nodded, cast her eyes down, and sighed. "Yes, I am. It's so sad."

"Yes, ma'am, it is. Federal and local law enforcement are currently searching both the river and lake for the young lady, and we are asking that everyone here at Quartz Creek campground remain in their RVs and/or tents for the next twenty-four hours. We are asking everyone to stay away from the lakeshore, and most especially, children." He glanced at his list. "You have two children, is that right, Ms. Waska?"

She nodded. "Yes, my daughter, Amka. And my son, Yutu."

"And, if I may ask, where are they right now?"

She thumbed behind her. "Amka is helping me finish the dishes. Yutu is out walking our Klee Kai."

Tightness gripped Luiz's chest. "How old is your son?"

"Twelve."

Luiz raised his head to try to hear a boy's voice, a dog's bark. Nothing. "Where did he take the dog, Ms. Waska?"

She shrugged. "He should be behind the RV."

Luiz nodded. He then stepped away and walked around to the back. The light of a clear moon helped him navigate through the darkness. He reached the back of the RV. There was no boy or dog.

"Yutu!" He shouted. A minute later, Yutu's mother stepped out of the RV. Luiz turned to her. "Call to your son."

"Yutu!" she shouted, cupping her mouth with her hands. "Yutu!"

Luiz called for him again and stepped closer to the edge of the tree line that extended into a thick underbrush. "Yutu!"

Then, he heard it: a faint voice, like a distant call. It echoed through the trees. Then, he heard the Klee Kai barking. Then, a boy's voice, not a scream really, more of a muffled whine, as if he were in pain.

Luiz drew his Glock 19M, pointed a finger at the mother. "Stay here. Keep your daughter safe."

He pushed through the underbrush, letting the light of the moon guide him. It was rough going. The leaves of spring had not fleshed out yet, but the bare branches were thick, unforgiving. He ignored them and kept going.

Now, Yutu's voice rose stronger, and so too, the dog's. The Klee Kai was barking, growling. The sweet singing voice that Luiz had heard a moment ago was now replaced by a shriek and a guttural hiss. Luiz pushed harder.

He stumbled into a row of trees, not too far from the SAR boat moored at the pier. The ground was soft, muddy. Luiz slipped, caught himself before falling face-first into the mud, and kept going. He did not shout the boy's name; he didn't want to risk alerting the creature — if it was a creature — threatening the child and the dog. Luiz pushed up a small hill, his pistol trained forward.

There they were, all three of them. Yutu, his dog, and a creature that Luiz had never before seen. From a distance, it seemed frail and thin, like a whisp of bark, hardly something to fear. Then, it arched its back to pull away from the Klee Kai nipping at its parka. Its eyes radiated in the faint moonlight; its long, dark hair glistened. It bared its teeth, shrieked again, and slashed out at the dog's muzzle. The Klee Kai yelped as the Qalupalik's claws found flesh, but the dog didn't run off. It got right back into nipping at its parka, barking, growling, trying to save its boy.

As for Yutu, Luiz could hardly see him, for the creature had tucked most of him into its *amautik*. Yutu's face was partially covered; the part that Luiz could see looked angelic, calm, as if the boy slept.

Luiz trained the gun on the Qalupalik. "Let the boy go!" He shouted, not knowing if the creature would understand him. "Let him go... now!"

The Qalupalik screamed but did not obey the order. It moved on all fours, toward the lake beyond the tree line. The Klee Kai again had a hold of its parka, but Luiz knew that that would not be enough. This was a powerful creature, even if what Sakari said about its dying were true. It could, if it wanted, kill the dog and be safely away with Yutu in minutes.

Luiz fired over the Qalupalik's head. He could not fire a shot directly at it, for fear of striking the boy. The shot did nothing.

He holstered his gun and ran toward them, his blood and anxiety up, leaving a bad taste in his mouth. He had to do something. He could not allow this creature to take another child.

He leapt, grabbed the parka, and pulled hard. He struck the ground near the Klee Kai. He nearly lost his hold on the garment as the Qalupalik tried pulling its way toward safety. The parka tore away, dropping Yutu on the ground with a heavy thud. Luiz reached up and grabbed the boy's leg and pulled.

The Qalupalik was on Luiz instantly, digging its claws into his shoulder, his arm. Luiz gritted his teeth and tried fighting it off, but it grabbed his neck and squeezed.

Luiz felt a trickle of blood down his neck. He grabbed its arms. They were cold, clammy, and slick with watery muck. Its face hovered near his own, its bared mouth nothing more than a smelly cave of jagged teeth and black tongue. It snapped out at him with those teeth, and Luiz forced his own hands onto its neck so that he could keep it from finding his jugular. God, but it was strong! *It might be dying*, he thought, *but it's still powerful.*

From Luiz's right side, the Klee Kai slammed into the Qalupalik and knocked it aside, tearing it away from Luiz's throat. The dog tried sinking its own fangs into the creature's arm, but it knocked the dog aside like a bug. It rolled onto its torn parka, scooped it up, turned, hissed, and then fled through the dark wood.

The Klee Kai recovered and chased after it, but Luiz didn't care, nor did he try to stop it. What mattered was that he was alive, and so was the boy.

Yutu lay at his side, cuddled up in a fetal position. Wounded, perhaps, and still loopy from the Qalupalik's sleep spell, but he was alive.

Thank God, he's alive.

Chapter Ten

"Only minor wounds, boss," Luiz said as he was being attended to by local EMT brought in to address his and the boy's condition. "Nothing to worry about."

It wasn't Luiz's wounds—indeed, minor—that troubled Chimalis.

"It's my fault," she said, shaking her head, mouth agape looking at all the wrecked equipment on the SAR boat. She was thankful, at least, that the Qalupalik had not damaged the hull. The vessel was still operable, but not its crew. All three were found dead, drowned, face-down in the lake.

My fault.

"Come on, Chimalis," Luiz said, using her first name. A rare thing, indeed. "How could you have known that it would cause so much destruction?"

"All this destruction and the *death* of three of our colleagues. This matters, Luiz. Once all this is over with, there will be an inquiry, an investigation."

And my career will be in jeopardy. She did not say that out loud, but it was true. Whenever agents died on a mission, and particularly on a VPA mission, there was always an investigation as to the nature of said deaths. And, since Chimalis was in charge of the matter, she'd be the focal point of the inquiry.

She could, at least, take comfort in the fact that the boy and his dog were safe. Yutu was sleeping in his parents' RV and being attended to by the EMTs. The Qalupalik's sleep spell would take time to dissipate, but he hadn't taken any damage, suffered any wounds. His Klee Kai had suffered some significant ones, unfortunately: claw slashes across his back, and a nasty cut across his muzzle. But he was alive as well and would mend in time.

Chimalis turned to Sakari. The old woman had, at least, the decency not to say, "I told you so." She had been most concerned with Luiz being here at Quartz Creek without additional security. *I should have listened,* Chimalis thought. But her lack of knowledge of the northern cryptids, coupled with her anxiety with being on this boat, in a lake, had made her sluggish, indecisive.

"We've been two steps behind this Qalupalik for too long," Chimalis said. She pointed at Sakari. "Are you still convinced that she is dying, despite all this destruction?"

The old woman nodded. "Yes, and even more so now. She is desperate. She is taking great risks to find additional food sources and expending a lot of energy to ensure that she isn't captured or killed."

An agent assigned to Chimalis' boat walked in. "Agent Burton. Senator Cooke is on the line."

He held out his cell phone. Chimalis took it.

"Senator Cooke," she said, in as calm a voice as she could muster. "What can I do for you?"

"You can start by toning down your investigation and not causing such a stir." His voice was beyond agitated. "Three agents drowned? The media is all over this, Agent Burton."

"Yes, and so what?"

"So what? My wife and I are having to answer questions about why the VPA is on the case. Why three agents have died simply searching the water for my daughter. Why a child and his dog have been attacked, and what attacked them. Why—"

"Senator Cooke!" Chimalis was out of patience. "Your daughter was abducted by a Qalupalik, plain and simple. And this creature will feed off of her to survive. If we don't find this beast, and soon, your daughter will drift to shore one day, nothing but a dried husk. You'll have a whole hell of a lot of explaining to do when that happens. Or, perhaps you'll simply bury that truth under the rug as well, diverting blame by claiming that the FBI could do nothing to find your daughter. Perhaps you'll even call for an investigation. All to hide the fact that you aren't one of those weirdo conspiracy theorists that believe in the bogeyman."

"How dare you talk to me like that. I'm a senator from—"

"I have one question for you, Senator Cooke. Do you, or do you not, want us to find Elisapie alive?"

There was a pause, a long pause. Chimalis thought perhaps she'd lost the signal. Then, Senator Cooke said, quietly, "Of course."

"Then get me resources. Get me an additional SAR boat and divers. And do it right now!"

She severed the connection and gave the cell phone back to the agent. Then, she said, "Get the boats ready to launch. I want full sonar sweeps of this lake—constant and round the clock. We're going after this bitch!"

Chapter Eleven

The blip on the green sonar screen was faint. Chimalis squinted to see it properly. "The Qalupalik?"

The agent running the sweep shrugged. "Maybe. It could be a school of fish. Hard to know for sure. It hasn't changed its course abruptly like a school of fish might do. It's kept pretty straight for the most part."

"It's the creature," Sakari said, standing next to Chimalis and staring at the screen. "It's going to its hiding place. It's got two children to feed on. It'll hole up there and wait us out."

Which was precisely why Chimalis had ordered Senator Cooke to get his political head out of his ass, talk to the Feds, and provide resources. The question now was simple: when would those resources arrive? Luiz was looking into that.

They watched silently as the boat drew closer to the blip. It faded in and out, and for a few seconds, the signal was lost. Then, it came back, faint but steady. This didn't surprise Chimalis. She'd never been on a SAR boat searching for cryptids with sonar, but these kinds of creatures were notorious for fouling up tracking devices.

"Slow us down just a little, please," Chimalis said to the agent, touching his shoulder firmly to accentuate her order, "but keep it in range."

The boat slowed until the blip was on the edge of the sweep. The agent kept the throttle steady, and they all stared at the screen for seconds, minutes. To Chimalis, it seemed like an eternity. There it was: all they needed to do was to just grab it, shoot a net out of the prow, and snatch it right up. Chimalis rolled her eyes. *If only we had such sophisticated equipment.*

The blip disappeared. They waited, waited. It did not return.

"It's gone to ground," Chimalis said.

"And it'll stay there to wait us out," Sakari said.

Chimalis shook her head. "Maybe, maybe not." She tapped the agent's shoulder. "All stop. Drop the anchor and maintain the sweep."

The agent killed the motor and brought the boat to a comfortable stop. Not so for Chimalis, however. Just being on the boat was uncomfortable enough. Having it sway to a stop put her stomach in her throat. She took a deep breath and swallowed, hoping to force down the acid sloshing around in her esophagus.

Luiz stepped in. "I've got good and bad news, boss."

"Tell us the good first," Chimalis answered.

"Senator Cooke has just finished speaking with SAC Halsey. We're getting additional equipment and manpower."

"Good."

"Another SAR boat has been ordered to Kenai Lake, with diving crew. In addition, they're bringing diver's knives, three HK P11 underwater pistols, and four spearguns."

"Excellent." Chimalis nodded. "What's the bad news?"

Luiz cringed. "It'll take at least twenty-four hours for their arrival. The boat is coming from Anchorage, but the divers are coming from Washington state."

Shit! "We don't have that kind of time. With the energy that that creature expended fighting off you and the dog it'll feed on those children until they are *dead*." Chimalis shot a quick glance at Sakari. "I know you said we had months to find them, but I don't believe that. We have days, maybe, and a twenty-four-hour delay is too long." She swallowed stomach acid, feeling the burn in her throat. "We've got to go down there. *I've* got to go down there."

"I'll go."

Chimalis looked at Luiz, shook her head. "No. You're still recovering from your previous encounter, remember?"

"Minor wounds, boss. I have diver training."

"So do I."

All VPA agents were required to take diver training, since so many cryptids of the Americas — and around the world — were aquatic. Even Chimalis had had that training. She barely passed.

"Yes, you have," Luiz said, "but you're the boss. We can't let the boss go down there and risk her life, can we?"

Chimalis chuckled and felt a little better. Her stomach settled. "But I have the knife." She put her hand on the hilt of the blade resting in its sheath at her waist. "You can't use it."

Luiz shook his head. "I'm not suggesting that I try to kill it. Agent Keen and I will go down there to find its hiding spot and, hopefully, the children. By then, the other SAR crew and their equipment will be here. You and they can take care of its elimination."

Chimalis walked away from the sonar screen and considered the idea. Waiting twenty-four hours for additional crew and resources was too long. They had to locate the Qalupalik's lair. In twenty-four hours, both children could be dead.

And yet, to put Luiz in that kind of danger. *I should go down there.* Indeed, she should, but the thought of it made her want to bend over and puke.

"Okay, Luiz," she said, "you and Agent Keen will go. But no attack. You go down there, you find its little cave, and you mark it. Understood?"

Luiz nodded. "Understood."

Chapter Twelve

Nipi's flesh shook as delicious energy radiated through her chest. She leaned her head back and closed her eyes. It felt so good! She could even feel the rough bite marks that the dog had placed on her begin to heal and close. She sighed in full contentment. *I could stay like this forever.*

She let her hands linger on the children's faces for a few minutes longer, then pulled away. *No. I cannot feed until they are dead. Not yet. Not until I leave.*

Where would she go? *Back where I came from.* The ocean, of course. Back to Resurrection Bay and then out to sea. The journey back there, however, required her to move a mile or so over land, from one small river to another, and another, until she could taste the brackish water of the bay and breathe freely again. Why had she ever come this far inland to feed?

The energy coursing through her soggy veins roused her curiosity on the matter, but it wasn't enough to give her full understanding. She had done many things in her life that she could not explain. None of that mattered now. What mattered now was getting away, and quickly.

The boat people were coming.

Their terrible, nerve-wracking sound waves were muted now that she was back in her cave. She could stay here for a long, long time and wait them out. She shook her head, tendrils of her quickly greying hair waving in front of her eyes, obscuring her view of the children's haggard faces. The boy was still fit; she had only fed on him a few times. The girl? Her lips were dry and drawn up, exposing her small teeth. Her hair had begun falling out. Her back bent and stiff. Nipi shook her head. No, she could not stay here much longer. *If only I had taken that third child. A strong, spirited young boy who would have given me so much energy.*

Nipi bared her teeth and growled. If only she had taken him. So, so close. A few feet more, and she would have gotten away. But, that damned dog and the human with that pistol had stopped her. When was the last time she had been thwarted from a capture? Nipi tried to remember. Years ago, if ever.

Nipi drank a little more from the boy, letting the girl have a rest. Three, perhaps four more feedings, and the girl would be dead. And how would Nipi carry them both back to where she had come? She could tuck the girl into her *amautik*; the boy she could tug along, and the lake flow would help guide them. It would be difficult, and Nipi would have to feed along the way. But she could do it.

She heard a splash, faint but not too far away. She instinctively pushed the children down and covered their legs with rocks to keep them from floating. She considered covering their whole bodies but refrained. She didn't have time. She had to find out what had made that sound.

She swam through the cave opening and out into the lake. The sound waves hit her like a block of ice, but she was strong now, having fed off the children. She could handle it, at least for a little while.

Another splash and Nipi wiggled her way across the lake bottom. She paused behind a large rock, or was it a boulder or an old hull from a discarded boat? Perhaps both. The object's cold, hardened surface was rough, nearly sharp. She used it to hide herself from what was coming.

A light. First faint, then stronger, stronger, until she could see exactly where it came from. Not the sun, for it was cloudy today. This was coming from a half mile, perhaps a full mile, from where she waited. A clear, focused beam projected from some infernal machine. She shuddered.

The boat people are here.

She could not let this happen. She could not let them find her children. They still had many adventures ahead.

Nipi bared her teeth and brandished her claws, drifted up into the lake water, and swam toward the intruders.

Chapter Thirteen

Everything was working properly on his suit. Oxygen levels were good; the wetsuit provided ample protection against the frigid water; his camera and light source were functioning properly. His comm link with the boss wasn't perfect, but adequate.

"Luiz," Chimalis said over a popping connection, "do you read? Is everything all right?"

Luiz nodded out of habit. He held his thumb up to his scuba buddy, Agent Keen, who lurked nearby. He tugged on the tether that kept him and Keen attached to the boat. "Everything is a-okay, boss. Ready to go."

"Very well," Chimalis said. "You may begin. And remember: no attacks. Your mission is to mark the location, nothing else. If you see the Qalupalik, you report it immediately, and then you and Agent Keen will be pulled back. Understood?"

"Understood."

"And Luiz?"

"Yes?"

A pause, then, "Be safe."

He thumbed again to Agent Keen, and they proceeded.

He had no intention of attacking the Qalupalik, although they both had spearguns attached to their waists. Luiz had received training in the use of various underwater weapons. He'd much prefer one of the pistols ordered and enroute to their location; they had more ammunition and could be fired rapidly.

"Based on sonar readings," Luiz said over comm as he and Agent Keen swam forward, their tethers tugging at their backs, "it dropped off radar about a quarter mile from this spot."

Agent Keen pulled a hand-held sonar device from his pack, tethered it to his arm, turned it on, and took the lead. "If its hidey hole is nearby, we'll find it."

Luiz followed. He gazed out into the cloudy water as he trained his light source forward. Optimal visibility was about twenty feet; beyond that, chaos. "Visibility is lousy, my friend. Let's maintain close proximity."

Agent Keen slowed so that they swam together, side by side. The lake bottom was rocky; it made sense, then, for this Qalupalik to settle around here. But where, exactly? With so much sediment in the water sloshing back and forth, it would be difficult even for the hand-held to get a good reading.

"You get anything yet?" Luiz asked.

"No, nothing," Agent Keen said. "I'll increase the intensity by a third."

"Maintain course," Chimalis chimed in. "Nice and slow. It's around here somewhere."

They moved forward another one hundred feet. As they swam, Luiz kept brushing his fins against the lake floor, much to his annoyance. One of his deficiencies as an agent, he realized, was that, when he was "in the zone" so to speak, when he was focused on more than one thing at a time, he had trouble coordinating body movement. Basically, he couldn't walk and chew gum at the same time. Not exactly, of course, but his body seemed to shut down when his mind tried to juggle too many things at once. This was one of those moments. Where is its lair? Will we find the children there? Is it in its lair? And if so, how easy will it be to flush it out? Will the spearguns prove useful if needed? Will the children die before we find them? A million questions rolled around in his big brain, and all Luiz wanted to do was to stop and think.

That's why Chimalis was better at these physical tasks than he. She could, and quite easily, walk and chew gum at the same time. But there was something wrong with her on this mission, and it was clear to anyone with eyes: the boss was afraid of the water. She turned three shades of white with every mention of her having to go into Kenai Lake. Why? Why was she so afraid? Luiz did not know.

"I've got something."

Luiz held up and turned to Agent Keen. "What have you got?"

Agent Keen flicked a switch on his hand-held, said, "I've got something... wait. No. Yes... I think I have it. I... spearguns! Spearguns!"

Before Luiz could even reach for his, something passed between them and struck them both. Luiz scrambled to keep his balance, to keep from striking the rocks on the bottom and puncturing his wetsuit.

Christ...

Agent Keen dropped his hand-held and tried reaching for his speargun, but the Qalupalik was on him, slashing and cutting, ripping great lines through his suit and biting his head. He screamed, and the tether on his back began to pull him upward toward the boat.

Luiz could hear Chimalis' frantic voice in his ear, but he did not respond. No time. He regained his balance and tried reaching for his speargun. He had difficulty finding it with Agent Keen's blood drifting through the water, making visibility even worse. He trained his light toward the Qalupalik.

What a monstrous creature it was. The glow of the light through the blood, its jagged teeth, its sallow, slimy skin, its coal-black eyes, its bloody claws as it raked and raked at Agent Keen's chest, all made Luiz recoil and tug at his tether line. Finally, he had the speargun in his hand. He fumbled with the trigger, his nerves, his rapidly beating heart keeping him from a secure hold on the gun.

The Qalupalik, seemingly content now with its attack on Agent Keen, turned toward Luiz. It pushed off Agent Keen's limp body, propelling itself upward toward Luiz whose tether line was pulling him quickly upward.

Luiz screamed through his comm, found the trigger of his speargun, and fired.

The shot clipped the Qalupalik's face. A glancing blow, one that slowed its movement as the tethers continued to withdraw, but not enough to make it flee. It fell back, bared its teeth, and widened its eyes as deep, dark blood wafted out of its wound. Then, it came at him again.

Luiz threw the speargun at the Qalupalik. It knocked it aside easily and reached for his legs. He tried kicking the creature, but its claws ripped holes in the wetsuit and through his flesh. Luiz screamed. He continued to kick at it but failed to drive it away. The Qalupalik reached for his foot, grabbed it, and tugged.

Luiz howled as he felt the bones and cartilage in his left ankle give way. Through his pain, he kicked even harder with his right foot, again and again. This time, he struck its face, a nice hit between its soulless eyes. It let go and fell back into the mucky water.

Both he and Agent Keen were finally pulled out of the water. Luiz ripped his mask off and screamed. He felt like passing out, the pain in his legs and ankle almost too much to bear.

Agent Keen was worse. He hung on his tether like a limp piece of meat, his wetsuit in tatters. They pulled him up first.

"Luiz!"

He looked up, and there she was, Chimalis, standing on the port side. He tried to smile, to signal that he was fine. But he wasn't, and no amount of hand waving would convince anyone.

"I'm hurt, boss," Luiz whispered, trying to raise and wave his hand. "I'm hurt bad."

Tourniquets were wrapped around Luiz's legs to keep him from bleeding out through the deep lacerations running from his knees down. His left ankle was broken. As for Agent Keen, he didn't make it. The only thing the Qalupalik didn't do to his chest was tear through his rib cage and rip out his heart. They were both evacuated via helicopter to Anchorage. Chimalis tried to keep from crying as she helped them put Luiz on the air ambulance, but the tears flowed freely, and not only for fear of his wounds.

"Okay," she said an hour later to Sakari and two agents who stood near a map of the Kenai Lake area tacked to a corkboard. It was cold on the deck, but Chimalis didn't care about that anymore. "My guess is that, since this creature has been fired at twice and was attacked by a dog, it won't wait it out at the bottom of the lake. It'll make break for it and head toward Primrose." Chimalis pointed to the campsite. "It'll take the water outlet there—Snow River—to Ferguson Lake, then over land for a mile or so to Bear Lake. Then to Bear Creek and on down to Resurrection Bay. Primrose is where I recommend that we converge."

One of the agents pointed to Kenai Lake and then ran his finger west. "She could head westward past Riverside Lodge, down these rivers to Skilak Lake. And then down more rivers to Cook Inlet."

Chimalis nodded. "It's possible, but I doubt it. It's weak, desperate, and carrying two children; and not very small ones, either. The way west is a longer route, despite the fact that it'll have to climb out of the water and lug them across land if it makes for Primrose. No. It's got to get out to the North Pacific Ocean as soon as possible." She looked at Sakari. "What do you think?"

The old woman took a moment to look at both routes.

"I agree with Agent Burton," Sakari said. "She'll head to Primrose and try to escape there."

Chimalis' phone vibrated. She pulled it from her pocket. "Yes?"

It was SAC Halsey. They spoke for a few minutes. Chimalis answered whatever questions he had for her as best as she could without snapping back or bursting into tears. It was difficult. Halsey wasn't happy; that was clear. Twice, Chimalis had to pull the phone away from her ear to keep from bursting a drum. "Yes, yes, sir. I understand. No, not Riverside. Primrose. Yes, yes, sir. No, you do not need to call in more VPA agents, sir. I can finish this job. Yes, I will… on my honor. I promise. Burton out."

A long, uncomfortable pause. Then, Chimalis forced a smile. "They'll be putting the new resources in at Primrose." She turned to the two agents. "Disembark and head, slowly, toward the campsite. Keep the sonar hot and let me know when she moves."

"Yes, ma'am."

An hour later, the Qalupalik appeared on radar, heading toward Primrose.

CHAPTER FOURTEEN

Chimalis stood at the bow pulpit of the boat, looking through the cold, dreary mist as they plodded toward the Primrose campsite. She needed to feel the cold air on her face to dry away the tears; or perhaps freeze them in place, as a reminder to everyone that she was incompetent, a failure.

"Is there something I can help you with, Chimalis Burton?"

Sakari's voice startled her. Chimalis turned, wiped away those freezing tears. She shook her head and turned back to the lake. "No, I'm fine. Just… planning the next move."

Sakari stepped closer. Chimalis could almost feel the old woman's breath on her neck. "You're afraid of the water, aren't you?"

No sense lying about it; what good would lying do now? "Yes, Ms. Kolit. I am."

"Why?"

"I don't want to tell you."

A pause, then, "You experienced an incident like I did, didn't you? In your youth. You lost a family member—a sibling, maybe? —to the water? To a creature, perhaps?"

"No. No creature." Chimalis turned toward Sakari, wiped her face again. "I didn't lose anyone, but it was during middle school. My science class went on a field trip one weekend to Maroon Lake in Colorado, not too far from Aspen. For a geography project. Sightseeing mostly, but for research as well. At that time, I wanted to be a scientist, perhaps even a geography major."

Chimalis moved away from the bow and stood near the starboard side. She pulled her coat together at her neck. Sniffling, she wriggled her nose in the cold wind. "We weren't permitted to swim in the lake, but a friend and I were just kids, you know? Rebellious, breaking the rules. A group of us were staying in a cabin. We snuck out at night. We planned to skinny dip in the lake. It was just us girls, so we didn't think anything would come of it, so long as we did it fast and got back to our cabin before any of our teachers noticed. We were having a great time. Splashing around, laughing. Too loud, perhaps, but again, we were bucking the system.

"We were about to finish up when my friend discovered this big boulder near the lake. She wanted us to dive off of it, at least once. I declined because I knew that the water wasn't very deep at that spot. If we dived, we'd probably hit rocks or something, get cut up badly. But she went off to do it anyway.

"So, what I did was swim over to where she wanted to dive to check out the depth. I went underwater, checked out the bottom. Some rocks, pretty sharp ones too, but it was deeper than I was tall, so I figured she'd be fine. Hell, I was even considering a dive myself. I told her it was fine, and I waited for her to jump.

"She did, near me, and splashed me nicely. I laughed as I was thrown back from her strike. And kept laughing until half a minute or so went by, but she did not come up. I waited, waited. I called her name, 'Katie! Katie!' She didn't respond. Then, I dove."

Chimalis cleared her throat, shook her head. "My calculations were wrong, dead wrong. My friend had struck one of the sharp rocks and got impaled right through her side." She swallowed, sniffed. "All that blood, and her trying to free herself from the rock, frantically losing air, nearly passing out. I screamed underwater and gulped a mouthful too, nearly choking, but I grabbed her and pulled, and I'm sure I tore something inside her. But I pulled anyway, and I finally got her free.

"In the end, she survived, but she lost a kidney, and it took her months to recover." Chimalis sniffled again, wiped her eyes. "I failed my friend. I gave her bad information, and she paid the price."

"You were a child," Sakari said, placing her hand on Chimalis' shoulder. "Children make mistakes. I know this very well."

"I was a failure," Chimalis barked, pulling away from Sakari's hand. "I lacked understanding of depth perception, and my friend nearly died. And now, every time I think about going into a lake or river, all I see are clouds of deep red blood and my friend wiggling on the rock like a fish on a hook. I know I'll have to go down there and face this creature. But, every time I think about it, my stomach turns over, my head gets dizzy. I don't know if I can succeed.

"I've been two steps behind this Qalupalik the whole damn time, and I've let my fear of the water cloud my judgment. I should have gone down there instead of Luiz. If I had, I'd have stabbed that bitch and the whole thing would have been over by now."

There was a pause. Chimalis wiped her face again and listened to the beeping of the sonar as it tracked the Qalupalik moving to escape. It was moving slowly. Understandable with all that cargo to carry. Moving slow was good in a way: it gave them time to get that third boat in the water and try to block her exit near the Primrose Campground. It was bad because she was carrying two children who were on the brink of death.

What am I going to do?

Sakari put both her hands on Chimalis' shoulders and turned her so that they faced each other. "Young lady, I am an *ungakok*, a shaman. There aren't many women shaman in my culture, but I'm one of them."

"I thought you were a voice coach."

Sakari nodded and smiled. "That too. Both professions have given me an insight into the human spirit, and right now, Chimalis Burton, your spirit is crying out for courage and strength. Let me help you find your courage."

She resisted the offer at first, but eventually, she nodded. It wasn't like she hadn't been in a trance before. In fact, she had been many times to gain strength or pertinent knowledge for a mission. But, most often, those rituals involved Zuni practices and spiritualism, something Chimalis felt comfortable with and understood completely. This? The notion frightened her, but she accepted anyway.

"Very well," Chimalis said, "but I'm not too knowledgeable about Inuit rituals and spiritualism. I'm not sure I'll fall into a trance very easily."

Sakari chuckled. "No, no, my sweet girl. I'm not putting you in a trance." She winked. "I'm going to make you sing."

CHAPTER FIFTEEN

"I must warn you," Chimalis said as she and Sakari stood facing each other, "I'm not a very good singer. I'm more of an investigator-type person."

"I don't want you to sing words, Chimalis Burton," Sakari said, staring intently into her eyes. "I just want to hear your sounds. The sounds you make will reflect your emotions, your feelings. Normally, throat singing is a game, where two ladies face off and throw sounds back and forth until one of them either breaks or begins to laugh. The other lady, then, is the winner. But not this time. This time, we will share our trauma with one another, and through that, we will, hopefully, begin to heal so that we — *you* — can do your duty."

Despite limited Internet service here on Kenai Lake, Sakari had shown Chimalis some samples of how throat music worked. It was, she had to admit, quite lovely in its own way. It was unusual to see women throw moans and groans at each other like grown men on the toilet, but combined with sweet chirps, high notes, low notes, rhythmic inhalations and exhalations, it created a beautiful sound, one that helped calm the raging anxiety in her memories.

Sakari grabbed Chimalis' arms, squeezed them gently, and said, "Are you ready?"

Chimalis breathed deeply and nodded. "Let's go."

Together, they closed their eyes. Sakari squeezed Chimalis' elbows again. Chimalis did the same. Sakari moved her arms back and forth, creating a rhythmic motion between them.

It began…
Mu-ma
Ah-ma

Mu-ma
Ah-ma
Mu-ma
Ah-ma
Mu-ma
Ah-ma

Now shifting, and faster…

Ha-ha-ha
Ha-na-na
Ha-ha-ha
Ha-na-na
Ha-ha-ha
Ha-na-na

Over and over, the shifts from one phrase to another grew faster until it was hard for Chimalis to keep up. She breathed quickly, sucking in air, and letting it out in rhythmic patterns, answering everything Sakari said, then shifting to guttural sounds as the old woman shifted, keeping pace, not wanting to lose this game — no, not a game — to someone decades older than she.

Sakari shifted to head voice, squeaking out sounds that almost made Chimalis laugh out loud. But she, instead, used her mirth as an answer to the high-pitched sounds, creating a rhythm that her mind fell into effortlessly. It was like a flowing river with rivulets where rhythms and patterns changed. Chimalis felt light-headed with all the fast-paced breathing. She wanted to drop, but Sakari squeezed her elbows tighter and shifted her sounds lower into chest voice. Chimalis followed.

Here, in the deeper register of her voice, Chimalis laid back in her memories and floated, as if she were in a lake and the water around her were notes, sounds, the rhythmic patterns of her life: a child of six, playing in the backyard of their Aspen home, wondering why father had a deep cut on the right side of his face; why mother didn't seem concerned about it, and in fact, seemed joyous; Chimalis, a young teenager of thirteen, just noticing boys, but all the boys in her school seemed so much younger, so much more immature; asking one to her middle school prom and being rejected; Chimalis at fourteen and on that field trip to Maroon Lake, watching her friend climb that boulder, Chimalis in the water below her, cheering her on…

No, not cheering her on. In fact, telling her *not* to jump, but if she did, "Jump over here, away from the rocks. Please?" But her friend didn't listen; she jumped in the wrong place, impaled by the rocks, and nearly bled out and died. *It wasn't my fault.* The memories were all clear to her now. *Not my fault at all. I told her where to jump, and she didn't listen. Didn't listen…*

A-hu-ra
Ha-ha-ha
A-hu-ra
Ha-ha-ha

Chimalis fell to her knees. Sakari fell with her but kept her grasp on her elbows and maintained the rhythm.

Chimalis saw the creature, the Qalupalik, floating in front of her like a feather atop the water. A hideous creature of slimy grey-green skin, flat face, jagged teeth, black, hollow eyes. Covered only in a parka with a pouch. There was no child in that pouch, so Chimalis knew right away that Sakari had not put her in a trance, that she was not looking directly at the exact Qalupalik that they were chasing. This was from her own mind, an image formed out of all she had seen, all she had learned about this Arctic creature from Sakari, from FBI documents, from hearsay. She wished she could see the children, Elisapie and Toklo. The fact that she couldn't scared her. Were they still alive? She didn't know for sure, but her instincts told her *yes, they had to be*. The children were not dead, or the Qalupalik would have dropped one or both of them along the way, and the sonar scan on the boat would have detected that. Both were alive, and Chimalis was thankful.

She did not need to see the children to realize that all this time, she had blamed herself for her friend's terrible injuries. Over the years, she had reconfigured the details of the event in her mind such that she had placed the burden of blame on her own shoulders, and this was why she had been so afraid of the water. *Water didn't betray me*, she thought as Sikari's rhythm changed again, higher pitched, and faster. *I betrayed myself.*

A-yoo-yaya
hu-ya-yo
A-yoo-yaya
hu-ya-yo

A-yoo-yaya
hu-ya-yo
"Enough!"

Chimalis pulled away and dropped to the deck. The image of the Qalupalik faded from her mind. All she felt now was exhaustion and the pain around her tailbone where she had fallen.

Sakari moved closer. "You did well, Chimalis Burton. I'm impressed, but you pulled away first. I win." She smiled and winked.

Chimalis smiled as well and raised her hand for assistance. "No, Sakari Kolit. I won."

Chapter Sixteen

The third SAR boat was put into the water at Primrose. Now, Chimalis had three boats to use to try to box in the Qalupalik and prevent it from reaching the mouth of Snow River and, potentially, slipping away. Additional divers had arrived as well, and so Chimalis was pleased.

More good news came to her in the morning. The hospital called and said that Luiz was doing well. His lacerations had been cleaned and sewn up, and he was already walking again. Painfully, but walking.

Even better news came when her cell phone rang. Chimalis couldn't help but smile when she heard that scruffy voice she knew so well. "Father de Seña. How the hell are you?"

The old priest coughed, then said, "I'm fine, Bluebird, fine. More or less. Back home now. Still coughing like a demon, but otherwise—"

"You and your stupid ailments. I could have used your help on my current assignment, you know. I'm like a duck out of water here."

A chuckle, another cough. "I know. Things have gotten deadly up there for you."

"You know?"

"It's all over the news."

Chimalis huffed. "Sad. Senator Cooke must be ripping his hair out trying to straddle that delicate political fence."

"Mhmm." A cough. "But he's had nothing but positive things to say about the FBI and the investigation. He's mentioned you, as well, by name."

"Chewing me out, I suspect."

"No, not at all. You're good at what you do, Bluebird. This mission, this creature, may be a bit foreign to you, but you'll do well. You always do."

Chimalis paused, cracked a smile. "I'm glad *you're* doing well, Father. The world would be a lesser place without you."

"And you too, sweetheart."

"Any words of advice?"

Another pause. Chimalis could hear Father de Seña breathing on the other end. Labored breathing, but not too labored. He was old, that was obvious, and there would come a time when his coughing, his breathing, would end. But not today. Today, he was still with her, and Luiz, and everyone working hard at the VPA. For that, she was most grateful.

"Yes… don't die."

It was Chimalis' turn to laugh. A loud, strong laugh, one that carried across the boat such that all the other agents stared at her. A nervous laugh, letting all her anxiety over the past several days rush out of her mind, her body. A laugh that felt so, so good.

"Thanks, you old fart. I love you too."

She hung up and walked out onto the deck to look across the lake. Out there, and not too far per sonar, was the Qalupalik. It was coming.

"Everything is in place, Agent Burton," one of the divers standing behind her said. "What are your orders?"

She turned to him and smiled. This time, with no anxiety. "Drop anchor, and let's go get it."

If she could, Nipi would drop down to the bottom of the lake and sleep, using her children for comfort. Burying herself under them, and perhaps that would give her some relief from the incessant drone of the sound waves that had been dogging her escape. Just a little nap, and afterward, she'd feed on them both and start moving again. Then, she would have the strength to carry them over ground and on toward the ocean. It was the only way.

Now she heard and felt two separate sound waves. A new boat had been put in the water, and its pitch higher and surprisingly in sync with the other boat's constant blare. The other boat, the one she had attacked and whose evil equipment she had destroyed, ran along as silent as the two children she now carried. *Oh, if all boats were like them,* she thought, diving lower to find tiny breaks from the sounds. *I'd be out to sea already.*

Nipi knew what she had to do. She could sense it. These boats, and the creatures aboard them, would not let her reach the Snow River easily. They'd fight her with everything they had, and Nipi had no idea what that meant. Putting more humans in the water? Yes, probably, and that would be the easy part. She had taken care of the last two without much concern, save for that one firing his spear at her and nipping her face. *Foul creature!* The wounds for that were now gone, thanks to the energy of the boy in her care. What else might they do? Hit her with sound waves to try to distract her, keep her off guard? Humans were clever that way.

She found a nice outcropping of rock. Not as prominent as she would have hoped, but it would do. She hoisted the boy child up and in front of her and pushed him forward until his back rested firmly against the rocks. Nipi then reached behind her and grabbed the girl by her hair and tugged until she was out of the *amautik* and floating. She then took the girl with both hands and swung her over so that she and the boy lay side by side.

Nipi couldn't help but smile. She had so rarely gone on an adventure with two children at once; perhaps one or two times before. What a delight! She so loved sharing her experiences with others, and these two children were very special.

She put her hands on their faces and drank, letting the energy again crawl up her arms and into her face, neck, and chest. Nipi smiled and closed her eyes. She would miss her feedings with these two, so young, vibrant, full of imagination and kindness. The boy? He'd last another three or four feedings. The girl? Maybe one, two more. The combination of both had given Nipi the kind of energy she had always wanted in life. But it was fleeting. In the midst of all this desperate flight, their essence was wasted on her old, brittle body. Tomorrow, she'd have to feed again. Would the girl child survive it?

The boats closed in. Nipi could hear them moving closer, closer. Engines were cut, but the sound waves persisted.

She pulled her hands away from their faces. The boy's cheeks were wrinkled, sunken. The girl's face was bone-like, her sweet, young skin drawn so tight as to scare Nipi herself. A ghost face, like so many of the children Nipi had taken on adventures in the past.

Nipi ran a long, black claw across the girl's face. *Do not despair, sweet child. We will finish our adventure. You will see the ocean, whether you are dead or not. I promise.*

Nipi tucked them in firmly under the rocks so that they would be safe and secure and await her return. Then, she pushed herself up and toward the three large shadows cast by the boats' hulls.

<h1 style="text-align:center">CHAPTER SEVENTEEN</h1>

The rhythmic throat music that she and Sakari had engaged in had worked well. Seemed to, at least. But now that Chimalis was in the water up to her waist, she felt that same burning anxiety that she had felt most of her life. *I can do this*, she mouthed to herself, hopefully not loud enough for those monitoring her every move, every word, to hear. In truth, she did feel better, but not as much as she had just ten minutes ago. No matter. This had to be done, and now.

All three SAR boats had moved to form a ring (more like a pyramid) around the area where the Qalupalik had last been detected on radar. They then stretched cable among all three boats, pushed out netting like closing a shower curtain, and set the sonar to its highest level, the idea being that both the netting and the sound waves would panic the creature and make it disoriented and incapable of fighting back. A good plan, in theory. But, Chimalis had been in this cryptid catching game for a long, long time. Sometimes the plans worked, and sometimes they didn't. Kenai Lake wasn't the largest lake in Alaska, but it was large enough, and this Qalupalik was tough, despite its age.

Tethers were in place. They offered Chimalis a diver's knife, but she refused. "I already have one," she said, tapping the spirit blade sheathed to her waist. She did accept a HK P11 pistol and a speargun. Her light source was affixed to her goggles; her air tank was strapped to her back and at full capacity.

Chimalis gave a thumbs up to the crew on her boat, and they lowered her down until she was fully immersed.

Two other divers were lowered into the water as well.

Chimalis felt warmer in her suit than she thought she might, the water being so cold despite temperatures on the rise. No ice, thankfully, which was a blessing in two ways: Chimalis herself didn't have to deal with it, and the Qalupalik couldn't rely on it. Chimalis took a deep breath and let bubbles from her breathing system float to the surface.

"Are we ready?" she asked the other two divers via their comm link.

"Ready," they said together.

Chimalis breathed deeply. She turned on the light source affixed to her goggles and made sure that both her pistol and knife were easily reachable at her waist, despite the skin-tight gloves on her hands. No problem at all.

Perfect.

Nipi matched the sound waves with singing of her own, first light and pleasant, then rapid and infused with anger. She wasn't trying to lure children onto the ice and take them on an adventure this time. This time, she was a predator, and they, her prey. She would not feed from them. The idea of feasting on adult human blood was offensive to her. Bitter and rank, not sweet, as a child's was. No. She would cut them down as she had the other humans who had dived into the water to seek her out.

Three dropped in. She could hear their splashing, despite the boat's powerful sound waves. Three shadows on the surface of the lake, now descending further, fanning out, light from their faces shining through the dark water, searching for her. From where she hid among the rocks and rotting tree trunks on the lake floor, their light seemed limited, incapable of seeking far into the flow to find her. *Good. Very good. They will not find me or my children. And their lights tell me right where they are.*

Using her hands, Nipi propelled herself from her hiding place until she was several feet beneath the first human. She looked up into the weak light source and waited until it and the human moved past her. The human seemed oblivious to her presence. Nipi smiled and pushed herself up, like a bullet, toward the diver.

Chimalis heard the screams of the agent to her right before she had a chance to respond. Over the comm link, she heard the agent fire his HK P11. She pointed her light source toward the agent and caught a glimpse of the Qalupalik, nothing but a grey-green flash through the roiling lake particulates. The light flashed across its long claws and glistened in its dark eyes. The beast lunged for the agent's legs, tearing and ripping at them just like it had done with Luiz. Chimalis yelped and called for the agent's tether to be extracted while he fired again. Chimalis raised her pistol toward the Qalupalik but did not fire. She could not risk hitting the agent.

Chimalis holstered her pistol and drew her knife, but the creature fled. She searched around her, letting the light source seek through the muck. Nothing.

"Pull him up!" she shouted through the comm. "Now!"

The agent, still howling in pain, was yanked out of the water.

"We need to dive lower," Chimalis said to the other agent on her left. "It's too easy for it to attack from below. Let's drop to the bottom, let it come at us from the sides. It'll be harder for it to take us out."

She hoped so, anyway. The speed at which the Qalupalik had attacked the first agent was terrifying. Chimalis's heart was beating rapidly, too rapidly, and she felt like fainting. As the tethers loosened to allow her and the remaining agent to drop quickly, she took a deep breath, focused her mind on the matter at hand, and thought of the dying young girl and boy below her. Tucked away in the rocks somewhere. *On the bottom, we'll be able to improve our defense and seek out the children.*

Hopefully…

These humans were so weak, so fragile. The thought of that gave Nipi joy. Even the gun that the human had pointed and fired did nothing; the darts simply streaked past her with no effect. *This will be easy. They will all be dead soon, and I and my children will be gone.*

But even as she gloried at the idea of a quick escape, she could feel the energy that she had felt so strongly just a few minutes ago bleeding out of her, and for a moment, Nipi thought about going back to the children and feeding. No. That would lead the humans straight to them. No. She had to attack again and soon.

The remaining two humans dropped quickly this time. Nipi spit a curse. On the bottom they could find where she had hidden the children.

I must attack them again… now!

"She's about thirty-two meters ahead of you," said an agent over the comm, "and moving fast."

"Back-to-back!" Chimalis said to her diving buddy. "Back-to-back. And ready your spear."

The HK P11 was in her left hand, the blade in her right. Not being an expert at swimming, Chimalis found it difficult to balance, the fins on her feet awkward and difficult to move quickly. Her buddy came up and took his position at her back, a wall of air bubbles escaping his breather. He clutched his speargun with both hands. "Ready."

Waiting, waiting. "To the right, about fifteen meters."

"I'll take the first shot," her agent buddy said, "and then you—"

"Quiet! Quiet!" Chimalis hissed. "Do you hear that?"

A pause, then, "What? What is it?"

Chimalis smiled. "Singing."

Nipi swam quickly toward the human holding the speargun, letting her music fill the water around her and drown out the dreaded sound waves emanating from the boats above. *Just a few more feet, and I'll—*

The human fired the spear. Nipi had dodged many spears in her life. This one was fast, or perhaps it was just because she was older now and the energy bled out of her faster than usual. Whatever the reason, she rolled left to avoid the shot, but the tip of the spear struck her arm, splitting the skin to the bone. It was the strongest shot that she had taken in a long, long time. She growled, letting her anger and pain overtake her song.

Can I be killed by a spear? Nipi did not have an answer to that. Her life had been so rarely challenged through the centuries. *Maybe I'll just fall into a deep sleep and heal myself, no matter the pain or damage.* Regardless, now was not the time for either option. The spear had struck her. It was painful. She was bleeding.

Nipi endured the pain and struck the human in the chest, knocking it backward. It tried firing its pistol at her, but Nipi grabbed the muzzle and tore the gun out of its hand. She dropped it and struck out at the human's neck, raking at its gear, ripping away the smooth, skin-tight fabric and the glass mask covering its face. The human tried beating her with its fists. Nipi ignored the pain of each blow and kept biting. She could taste the human's blood with each bite. It was warm and comforting, but not life affirming. It held no energy; at least, not the kind that Nipi needed right now.

The tether yanked upward, and Nipi tried holding on as the cord pulled the wounded human to the surface. Then, she felt a pain that she had never felt in her life.

She turned. The human that she had ignored wavered there in the water, the light emanating from its facemask trained on Nipi's legs. Nipi looked down, and there, sticking in her left leg, was a knife held by the human.

The cut burned as if she were on fire. Light from the blade began to leach up her leg, turning her grey-green skin a pale blue. Nipi shrieked and struck out with her wounded leg, striking the human in the face and pushing it backward.

The blade fell out of her leg, and Nipi swam.

I must get to my children, she thought as she tried ignoring the excruciating pain from the strike. A pain that eclipsed any other pain in her body, even her hunger for energy. She needed energy *now*. The wound from that blade was something that she had never felt before, nor did she ever want to feel it again.

I'm dying. It was obvious now. The cut from that blade made everything so clear. *I'm dying. But maybe I have a chance… one more chance.*

Dammit!

Chimalis grabbed her knife before it reached the watery muck on the lake bottom. Once the blade had punctured skin, it was rare for a cryptid to be strong enough to pull away. This one may be old, but it wasn't without power. The strike had done some damage, thankfully; that was clear to Chimalis as she strengthened her hold on the blade and her HK P11. Enough damage to make the Qalupalik flee, perhaps back to where she had hidden the children.

She chased after it, losing distance as the Qalupalik moved swiftly to put space between them. The light affixed to Chimalis' mask, fortunately, was still bright enough to keep the creature's feet and legs in view. One leg that, even through the winding particulates of the water, still bled. Bleeding out her essence, her strength. Chimalis couldn't help but smile behind her mask. There was no doubt now where the Qalupalik was headed.

Her legs tired, her muscles aching to keep pace. Not only was the creature fast, but Chimalis had to tug on the tether periodically to draw more line. That slowed her down even further. She considered dropping the pistol and using her free hand and arm to propel herself forward by pushing off slimy rocks. Chimalis shook her head. If this cryptid was strong enough to reject the blade, then she'd need all the firepower she could muster.

"She's stopped," said the comm message from the boat.

"Do you have her exact location?" Chimalis asked.

"No, but she's within ten, twenty meters of you. Be careful, ma'am."

Chimalis suddenly wished Luiz were on the boat and not at the hospital. She wished she had a direct comm link to him. 'Be careful, boss,' is what he would have said, and oh, how she needed his support right now. Her hands shook. Her heart raced wildly in her chest, but she didn't feel like fainting anymore. That, at least, was progress.

She holstered her pistol and dropped a little lower to use the uneven lake floor as a shield. She paddled her fins slowly, eyes focused forward. She didn't bother looking left or right to see if the Qalupalik would flank her. It wouldn't. The creature had stopped right where she had hidden the children. Chimalis was certain of it.

There it was. Chimalis let her light source rest on the face of the creature. It did not move. Its eyes were closed, and it had a small, pleasant smile on its cold, flat face. Its arms were outstretched. Its hands rested on the children's faces.

She reached for her HK P11 and drew it. The Qalupalik slammed its eyes open, saw the move, squeezed the children's faces, and turned such that they stood as a barrier between it and Chimalis.

Fire the gun, a little voice in Chimalis's mind called out. *Take the shot.*

But the children were in the way, two drawn, sallow-fleshed children who looked dead already. Chimalis wanted to cry, wanted to blow the head off this Qalupalik for what it had done to them.

Take the shot!

Not possible. All three faces were too close together. Even if she aimed directly at the middle face, the recoil of the gun, the water current, a million little things might force the dart to deviate just enough to strike the boy on the left or the girl on the right. Instead, Chimalis holstered the pistol and sheathed her blade, put up her hands as if she were surrendering, and began to sing. To hum, really, through her breather and comm link.

"What are you doing?" asked the agent on the other end. "Ma'am… what's going on?"

Chimalis didn't answer. She kept humming. Could the Qalupalik hear her? She did not know, but she kept singing all the same, her eyes fixed directly on the creature's face. She sang in the same rhythm and pattern that she and Sakari had sung on the boat just a day ago. It was difficult to maintain the rhythm due to her breather, but she worked through it. Inhale, exhale. Head voice, chest voice. Again and again, until she felt light-headed, wanted to stop, but she kept breathing and singing.

The Qalupalik released the children and began to answer Chimalis' song.

They seemed to float toward one another. Chimalis hesitated at first, worried that she had made a grave mistake doing this. The Qalupalik's dark, vacuous eyes were almost mesmerizing as it drifted toward Chimalis. The creature extended a hand. Chimalis balked then reached out.

They touched. Chimalis could not feel the creature's skin through her gloves, but there was a warmth that emanated from the Qalupalik's hand despite the bitter cold water around them. To Chimalis, it felt good, almost inviting, and she squeezed the frail hand with its long, black fingernails as if she were holding her own mother's hand.

Now they sang together, Chimalis adding a phrase and the Qalupalik answering. Back and forth in greater speed than when she had sung with Sakari. The creature was exceptional, far better than Chimalis would ever be, its voice pitch-perfect with whatever sounds Chimalis managed to blurt out. They were in perfect harmony, and it seemed to Chimalis that the Qalupalik was telling its life story. The day it was born; the day it foolishly wandered out onto a frozen lake and saw a face below the ice; the first child it had taken as a Qalupalik; the next and the next; the near-death experience with whalers who had captured it in their net; its valiant escape from scores of near-death moments; the joy of feeding on young, vibrant energy; the sadness of seeing each and every one of its children breathe their last breath; the sadness of all of its adventures coming to a close; the painstaking need for more and more feedings, especially in these last few years; the painful realization that it was not immortal and that the end would come someday, perhaps today; the instinctive need to transfer its own life force to someone else—

Chimalis stopped singing, drew her HK P11, squeezed the trigger, and sent a dart through the Qalupalik's chest. The creature stopped singing and recoiled back from the shot, but Chimalis held its hand tightly. She then dropped the pistol to draw her blade, and drove it into the Qalupalik's throat.

The creature howled. Even through her equipment, the scream hurt Chimalis' ears. But the blade remained firmly in place, and no amount of motion would dislodge it now. Not even the Ahayu'da, the twin Zuni Gods of War, could pull it away. It was set, and into its blade and handle, the Qalupalik melted.

It drifted into the blade, one inch at a time, as if it were a pixelated image on a computer screen. It shimmered, shook, its grey-green skin bursting with light, and then, as if being pulled down a drain, its body collapsed into the blade, sucked into a vortex, swirling around and around the knife until there was nothing left, save for a small, bright icon burned into the handle. Chimalis grabbed the blade before it fell away. It was hot, even through her gloves, but it was steady, whole, and intact. She smiled. Then, she remembered why she was really here.

The children.

She tucked the knife away and scrambled to find them. She trained her light toward the bottom, and there was the boy, head down, feet pointed toward the surface as if he were a book leaning on a shelf. His leg jerked. *He isn't under a spell anymore*, Chimalis realized. *He's going to drown.*

But where was the girl? Senator Cooke's daughter? Chimalis grabbed the boy's leg and tugged him along as she scanned the lake floor. She turned her head left, right, up, down, scanning every inch of water and rock. *Where is she?*

There she is. Chimalis' heart leapt into her throat, and in her excitement and relief, she almost dropped the boy.

Elisapie was cuddled up like she was sleeping, wedged between two rocks. But she wasn't sleeping. She was struggling. Her body jerked. The girl's eyes opened. She bared her teeth in fear, to scream.

Chimalis grabbed Elisapie and pulled hard, tearing away a portion of her sleeve. The girl's exposed arm tore against the rock, but Chimalis kept pulling until the girl was out and in her arms.

"Up! Up!" Chimalis screamed into the comm. "Pull us up… *now!*"

Chapter Eighteen

Chimalis crested the top of the lake. She lifted the children up as she did so.

"I've got them. Pull us in. They're dying!" she screamed into the comm.

The tether extracted, pulling all three against the boat and up until the cable stopped. Agents reached over the railing, grabbed the children, and pulled them up. Chimalis ripped off her goggles and breather. "They need oxygen, now!"

Another agent helped Chimalis over the railing. When she was steady on the deck, she pushed him away and went to the children's sides.

The boy didn't seem too damaged. His face was drawn. He struggled to breathe, but he wasn't too withered, too broken. EMTs took him immediately, checked his vitals, and began to pump his chest and breathe air into his mouth. As for Elisapie…

She was in deep trouble. Her eyes were sunken; her face drawn and tight. She wasn't breathing. EMTs were on her quickly as well, checking her vitals, pumping her chest, feeding her oxygen. Chimalis moved up slowly and put her hand on the girl's shriveled leg.

She never prayed much, but Chimalis called now — to Earth Mother, Sun Father, and many kachinas — for the girl's life, her safety. She was no Qalupalik (thank the gods!), but she tried imparting her life force into Elisapie, to give her a part of her own strength. *Come on, sweetie,* Chimalis mouthed to herself. *Come back to us.*

The boy, lying several feet away, coughed violently for a few seconds. Then, he began to cry.

The EMTs continued to work on Elisapie, over and over, neither of them willing to give up. Chimalis leaned in, gripped the girl's legs, perhaps harder than she had intended. *Please, Earth Mother, Sun Father, bring her back. I will give my life for hers. Bring her back. Bring her —*

The leg moved. Again, then again. Elisapie coughed, moved her leg again, then began to cry. Her eyes opened, and she looked around her as if she had been awakened from a dream, a nightmare. She spit up water, coughed, looked at Chimalis with wide, terrified eyes and said, "Is my adventure over? Is it over?"

Chimalis did not know what Elisapie meant, but she smiled, nodded, and said, "Yes, sweet girl. Your adventure is over."

The EMTs carefully picked up the girl and carried her away. Chimalis let her tears flow as Sakari appeared, knelt, and gave her a strong hug. Chimalis hugged her back.

"You did it, Chimalis Burton," Sakari said helping her to her feet. "You did it."

Chimalis nodded and laid her head on the old woman's shoulder. "No, Sakari Kolit. We did it."

Sakari squeezed tighter. "Come, let's get you inside the cabin, get you warm."

Chimalis resisted. "No, I'm okay. I'll stay out here. I need the air." She paused, then said, "Can you get me a blanket and some hot tea, please?"

"Of course," Sakari said and walked into the cabin.

Chimalis stood there, watching the EMTs continue to administer treatment to Elisapie and Toklo in the cabin of the boat. There, they would also be prepped for a helicopter waiting at Primrose for quick transfer to an Anchorage hospital.

Senator Cooke and his wife would be very pleased with the result, though there was no guarantee exactly how Elisapie would survive. In time, she would recover fully. Physically, she was weak, frail, malnourished. It would take weeks, perhaps months, for her to fully recover physically. Mentally? Who could say? It all depended upon how much the young girl remembered of her abduction and the time she had spent submerged under Kenai Lake. The trauma of the experience might last months, years, perhaps a lifetime. Just like Chimalis's own trauma at that campsite in Colorado all those years ago.

But Elisapie was alive. So too, Toklo. And that mattered.

Chimalis walked to the railing and leaned into it. The air was cold and wet. The sky was dark. Thick grey clouds gathered. Snow and ice seemed imminent. She'd be happy when this was all over, when she was back in Denver, in Aspen, writing her full report, in the comfort of her office, her home, with Luiz at her side.

She reached for her belt and plucked her knife from its wet sheath. It was still warm. She opened her palm to see the handle, and there, etched into the thick, dry leather, was an image of the Qalupalik. A small, glowing image, almost too small to see clearly. It looked almost like a mermaid, a Greek siren. But that did not matter. What mattered was that the creature had been vanquished, the children had been saved, and life would go back to normal along Kenai Lake.

For a while, at least.

Chimalis gripped the warm handle. She looked out over the surface of the water, smiled, and hummed a song.

Robert E Waters is a technical writer by trade, but has been a science fiction/fantasy fan all his life. He's worked in the computer and board gaming industry since 1994 as designer, producer, and writer. In the late 90's, he tried his hand at writing fiction, and since 2003, has sold over 7 novels and 80 stories to various on-line and print magazines and anthologies, including the *Grantville Gazette*, Eric Flint's online magazine dedicated to publishing stories set in the 1632/Ring of Fire Alternate History series.

Robert's first 1632/Ring of Fire novel, *1636: Calabar's War*, (co-authored with Charles E Gannon), was recently published by Baen Books. Robert has also co-written several 1632 stories, including the Persistence of Dreams (Ring of Fire Press), with Meriah L Crawford, and The Monster Society, with Eric S Brown.

Robert is the author of The Mask Cycle, a Baroque fantasy series which includes the novels *The Masks of Mirada* and *The Thief of Cragsport* (Ring of Fire Press).

For e-Spec Books, Robert has written several stories which have appeared in the widely popular military science fiction anthology series, Defending the Future. All seven of his stories which appeared in the series were recently collected into one volume titled *Devil Dancers*.

Robert currently lives in Baltimore, Maryland with his wife Beth, their son Jason, and their two precocious little cats, Snow and Ashe.

ABOUT THE ARTIST

Although Jason Whitley has worn many creative hats, he is at heart a traditional illustrator and painter. With author James Chambers, Jason collaborates and illustrates the sometimes-prose, sometimes graphic novel, *The Midnight Hour,* which is being collected into one volume by eSpec Books. His and Scott Eckelaert's newspaper comic strip, Sea Urchins, has been collected into four volumes. Along with eSpec Books' Systema Paradoxa series, Jason is working on a crime noir graphic novel. His portrait of Charlotte Hawkins Brown is on display in the Charlotte Hawkins Brown Museum.

artist's rendition of Qalupalik

Qalupalik

(Also Qallupilluk or Qallupilluit)

Origins: A creature of the Artic, this cryptid is said to live deep in the ocean, hunting along the shores, moving among the ice floes and perhaps even inland waterways looking for opportunities to hunt among the Inuit people. Some call this aquatic creature, said to snatch children coming too close to the shore, their version of a mermaid.

Description: Though accounts cite both male and female pronouns, these cryptids are most commonly referred to in the feminine manner, described as having bright eyes, fierce teeth, long hair, and slimy greenish-blue skin with bumps and scales. Their hands are webbed and possess long, claw-like finger nails.

Despite the purity of their salty ocean home, this water-dwelling bogeyman reeks of sulfur. According to accounts, they snatch children into the water with their long, thin arms, shoving them into the pouch of their amautik, an Inuit parka usually worn by women, with a pouch on the back. It is not known for certain why they snatch children. Some believe it is to devour them, others believe they are kept as companions, and yet others believe the creature steals their life force to maintain its immortality.

In their hunt, they are said to use sound, either an ethereal hum to lure their prey or a shrill noise produced by one of their two flippers to paralyze their victims. It is also believed that they possess an ability called pilutitaminik that allows them to alter their appearance to that of a seal or a whale, or perhaps other forms.

According to lore, in its true state, this creature is invulnerable, but can be killed when transformed into another form, which clever hunters have been known to use to their advantage.

Life Cycle: the origin of this marine creature is not known nor how it reproduces, but lore says this cryptid is cursed with immortality.

History: There are accounts going back centuries of those who have lost their lives in the embrace of these native cryptids. The skeptics are of the opinion that the elders merely warn the young away from the shore to keep them from falling through thinning ice, and that the noises heard were the ice cracking and buckling. Others are certain that the water's surface hides a predator waiting for unwary children to draw within reach, betrayed only by a knocking sound traveling across the ice.

But what if there is no ice? It is said that if the free-flowing water is wavy or steam rises from the surface, one of these creatures may be lurking beneath the surface.

All is not about the hunt, however. There are accounts of children willfully being surrendered to this creature by their loved ones because they could not feed them, and it was believed their lot would be better. One account has a young couple searching for one such boy, seeking to retrieve him once food was plentiful again. It is said they found him tethered by a strand of seaweed so he could not flee. They could not free him at first, but waited until dawn and were able to sever the bond.

VARIANTS: Mermaid, Siren, Kappa

Capture the Cryptids!

Cryptid Crate is a monthly subscription box filled with various cryptozoology and paranormal themed items to wear, display and collect. Expect a carefully curated box filled with creeptastic pieces from indie makers and artisans pertaining to bigfoot, sasquatch, UFOs, ghosts, and other cryptid and mysterious creatures (apparel, decor, media, etc).

http://CryptidCrate.com